The Guestbook at Asilomar

The Guestbook at Asilomar

RJ Stastny

THE GUESTBOOK AT ASILOMAR

iUniverse books may be ordered through booksellers or by contacting:

iUniverse
1663 Liberty Drive
Bloomington, IN 47403
www.iuniverse.com
1-800-Authors (1-800-288-4677)

Cover photo by RJ Stastny
Graphic editing and effects by Shara Gardner, Adept-Graphics.com

ISBN: 978-1-4917-4261-7 (e)
ISBN: 978-1-4917-4262-4 (sc)

Library of Congress Control Number: 2014914252

Printed in the United States of America.

iUniverse rev. date: 9/15/2014

Dreams

Hold fast to dreams
For if dreams die
Life is a broken-winged bird
That cannot fly.

Hold fast to dreams
For when dreams go
Life is a barren field
Frozen with snow.

—LANGSTON HUGHES

Contents

Acknowledgments

I want to thank Eric Littles for kindly answering my many questions regarding Deaf culture and Maurice Carter for providing his unconditional support and encouragement.

Quiero dar las gracias a mis queridos amigos en España por haberme ayudado a crear un entorno especial y acogedor para escribir.

"Dreams" from The Collected Poems of Langston Hughes by Langston Hughes, edited by Arnold Rampersad with David Roessel, Associate Editor, copyright © 1994 by the Estate of Langston Hughes. Used by permission of Alfred A. Knopf, an imprint of the Knopf Doubleday Publishing Group, a division of Random House LLC. All rights reserved. Any third party use of this material, outside of this publication, is prohibited. Interested parties must apply directly to Random House LLC for permission.

Prologue: Of Dreams

The glass of ice-cold lemonade in Morris's hand gave him the illusion of refreshment but did little to distract him from the fact that it was summer in the desert. The thermometer that hung in the shade of an old mesquite tree registered 117 degrees. Wearing only shorts and a tank top, he reclined on the chaise lounge. His eyes panned across the garden. The ripples of heat shimmered over the yard that consisted mostly of sand and rocks. Not a creature stirred, as none was brave enough to venture out from its protective hiding place. With limited success, he had spent years trying to create an oasis of flowering trees and shrubs in an otherwise hostile environment. It was the desert, after all, and any attempt to cultivate it was not only difficult but almost unnatural.

As he rested he heard a rumble overhead. *Right on time,* he thought. As he looked skyward, a 747 jumbo jet came into view. It had taken off from McCarran Airport in Las Vegas and followed the usual flight pattern to the west before making a 180-degree turn away from the mountains. It then headed east on a route that would take its cargo of adventurers on a nonstop journey to Europe. Even from inside the house he could hear its distinctive rumble. He would often step outside just to watch the giant bird whisking the hundreds of lucky travelers on a voyage for which he had long awaited.

The jet and its noisy wake faded into the distance. Beads of sweat rolled down his cheek. The gentle breeze offered little relief and instead covered him in a blanket of hot desert air. He took a long sip on the straw, hoping to enjoy the coolness of his drink before the ice cubes lost their battle against the heat, a battle to which he had already surrendered.

He blinked several times as his eyelids struggled to stay open.

Fears and Doubts

Maurice was thrust against his seatback as the four engines of the 747 revved up to full power, propelling the beast of a plane down the runway. He took a final glance down the aisle and made brief eye contact with a flight attendant who had taken a crew seat that faced toward the back of the plane, where he was sitting. She acknowledged him with a courteous smile.

He took a deep breath and became conscious again of the signature airplane smell that caught his attention as soon as he boarded. He likened it to a combination of diesel fuel, old luggage, and Febreze. Regardless of its composition, its association with a fear of flying brought beads of sweat to his forehead.

With his head pressed against the seat, he turned toward the window and saw the terminals rushing by. The engines grew louder, and the vibrations of the jet rolling down the runway shook the overhead compartments. The bottles and glasses were clanging noisily in the galley behind him.

Although the race down the runway lasted only a few moments, it seemed as though time temporarily had stopped. So many thoughts raced through Maurice's mind. He momentarily felt paralyzed, and his senses of sight, hearing, and smell were temporarily suspended.

In just a few short seconds, the vibrations stopped, but the engines continued to roar, keeping him pressed against his seat.

1

The jumbo jet had broken free of the gravity that kept it bound to earth. Perhaps it was a fitting metaphor for Maurice, having broken free from the inertia that kept him housebound for so long. For him, being on this flight was a minor victory in confronting the separation anxiety that had prevented him from leaving his insulated and protected little world. Although it was just a two-week trip, it challenged many of the self-created obstacles that kept him bound to a dull routine: a lack of confidence in making decisions, the fear of flying, the risk of losing his job, and, most of all, the anxiety of leaving all that was familiar. When all else failed, he would use his dog as an excuse for having to stay home. Although he took the time off against his boss's wishes this perpetual daydreamer knew he needed a change of scenery. While he struggled to free himself from the inertia of home life, he longed for the enthusiasm and energy that he admired in his friends. He was starting to feel older than his thirty-three years. The gray hair he discovered on his lightly bearded face that morning didn't help the argument.

There was an eerie quiet in the plane cabin except for the loud hum of the engines. Maurice had requested an aisle seat so he could stretch his legs and walk about the cabin without disturbing anyone. He was fortunate that the window seat next to him was vacant. Fighting the force that kept him pressed against his seat, he leaned over and again peeked out the window. He could see the highways and the hotels on the Las Vegas Strip disappearing below him. After a few moments the jet started to bank to the right, making a wide turn as it continued to climb. He watched as the mountains disappeared, always a familiar and reassuring part of his home landscape. He hoped his fears and self-doubt would fade and be left behind, as well.

"Damn," he said softly. "I'm finally doing it."

Maurice was a frustrated writer. While his job paid very well, he was bored and felt that his creative talents had become dull from the ten years of writing business articles for a local magazine. Staying at home did nothing to provide him the inspiration to breathe excitement into his writing ... or into his life, for that matter. He didn't have much luck in the romance department either. After a series of bad relationship choices, he burrowed deeper into his self-made world—his "self-exile," as friends would call it. Although he considered himself a loner and didn't mind spending time by himself, he had come to realize that the world he had created for himself was hollow. Outside of several close friends he had little social life. One of his friends teased him that he was becoming an "Oblomov," a character inspired in Russian literature who was incapable of making important decisions or undertaking any significant actions.

But Maurice wasn't lazy. He was athletic, worked out at the gym, hiked, and worked in the garden. It wasn't for lack of dreams or imagination that he confined himself to his little world. This perpetual daydreamer would drift off wherever he might happen to be, staring, lost in thought. He once wrote that his dreams were in color but his life was in black and white. He couldn't remember when he last felt a surge of excitement. What to him seemed courageous and risky was to others merely a matter of enjoying life's great experiment.

It wasn't until after months of prodding that his close friend Sheila convinced him that he was wasting his life and needed to do something impulsive. She suggested that he plan a little adventure somewhere far from his familiar surroundings.

Maurice rested his head against the seat as the plane continued its ascent. He felt his body tingling, perhaps some of it due to nerves, but there was something else that he hadn't felt in a long while—a cautious excitement. He wasn't daydreaming this time. He was in pursuit.

His plans were to fly to Madrid, Spain, and then drive south to the Andalusian city of Granada, where he spent his junior year abroad at the university. He figured he could spend a couple of weeks getting reacquainted with his favorite city in Spain, brush up on his Spanish, and revisit some of the significant moments of his young adulthood, including his first sexual experience. He had arranged most everything ahead of time, reconfirming hotel and car rental reservations several times. He had rehearsed schedules and travel routes in his mind. As he sat still in his seat, he had already begun visualizing his arrival.

Maurice's daydreaming was interrupted by the intercom. A flight attendant was making her first announcement. "Welcome to Virgin flight 5330 nonstop to Madrid. Our flying time will be approximately ten hours and twenty minutes. Very shortly the captain will be turning off the seat belt sign and we'll be offering beverages and several meal choices …" Her announcement continued, but Maurice suddenly remembered there was a bag of chocolates in his carry-on bag that he needed. He started to get out of his seat.

"Excuse me, sir, please remain seated until the seat belt sign is off." The flight attendant had one hand on her hip and the other pointing to his seat.

"I'm sorry, but there's just something I wanted to give—" Maurice started to reply.

"I'll be back in a few minutes to answer your questions, sir, but please take your seat until we level off."

Maurice returned to his seat, pushing his red-framed glasses back into place on the bridge of his nose. He understood that she was just trying to get the passengers settled down for the long flight ahead, and he was embarrassed that he had drawn attention to himself.

He was eager for the beverage service to start. He wasn't a good flyer and had already washed down a Valium at the airport cocktail lounge before boarding. Even though it was a long overseas flight, he didn't expect to get much sleep.

He fumbled in his seat, running his hand under his legs and behind his back. He stuck his hand in the seat pouch in front of him. It wasn't there. Then he noticed on the floor by his feet there was a pad of paper with a pen clipped to one of the pages. It must have fallen off his lap during takeoff. Maurice was an avid note taker. He'd jot down observations and random thoughts, some simple and others more profound, or so he'd like to imagine—anything, he thought, that might come in handy someday for a future writing project, maybe even a novel. He dreamed of one day being a respected and well-known author. The irony was that while he dreamed of fame, he was introverted and shy. Whenever he had traveled in the past, it had been with a friend, usually someone who was more outgoing. Maurice would do most of the planning and let his travel companion introduce them to locals and other fellow travelers they might encounter.

As he reached down to pick up his pad and pen off the floor, he couldn't help but glance across the aisle. A very young boy, probably no more than ten or eleven years old, was looking at him. At first he ignored the boy's intense stare.

Maurice scrolled through the first few pages of his notepad, relieved that it was recovered and intact. Although he was a writer of feature stories for a business magazine, most of his notes were personal and unrelated to his job. He had become accustomed to jotting these down on his iPad, but he figured on the plane it would be easier to do it the old-fashioned way.

He made a short entry on the notepad.

He no sooner finished a couple of sentences when he felt a tug on his sleeve.

"Hey, mister, what are you writing?" It was the little boy across the aisle. He had a curious, if not mischievous, grin and sported short spiked hair that looked out of place on a youngster his age. "Can

I see it?" he insisted. He reached out his little arm, as if expecting Maurice to surrender his valuable pad of paper.

"Well, little man, it's nothing special. Just some notes to myself." Maurice was trying to be nice but didn't want to spoil the moment trying to explain what he barely understood himself.

"My name's Calvin. Can I read it? Let me see it, please?" The boy was relentless. "Is it a letter to your mother? My mom always tells me I have to write her when I go away."

"No, Calvin. It's not a letter. It's just some stuff I write down so I don't forget it," he explained.

"Like errands your mother told you to do?"

Maurice soon realized that every answer only helped to generate another question. A lady whom he assumed was his mother appeared sound asleep next to him.

"No, just things I'm thinking about," he replied, trying to keep the conversation as simple as possible.

"Gosh, you must forget a lot," Calvin said with a sympathetic look on his face. "My mom says my dad was stupid 'cause he had to write down everything or he'd forget. I don't have my dad anymore."

That last statement made Maurice feel a little guilty that he had become irritated by Calvin's unintended invasion of privacy.

The young boy continued to stare at Maurice.

"Hey, are you a teacher?"

Maurice chuckled. "No, I'm not a teacher."

"You look like one," said the boy.

Maurice wasn't feeling in the mood to engage Calvin anymore and looked away to make another entry on his notepad.

"What are you writing?" the little voice asked again.

"Things I observe." Maurice didn't look up, with the hope that Calvin would give up.

"Why?" Calvin persisted.

Maurice rolled his eyes but tried to remain pleasant. "I want to write a book, and sometimes it's hard to remember everything when you're busy." Maurice then realized that, except for a close friend, this little boy was the first person with whom he shared his goal of being an author. Disappointed at first that he gave away his little secret, he felt a bit liberated having acknowledged out loud for the first time his dream of writing a book. It was also comforting that his secret would likely be safe with little Calvin.

Fortunately, the window seat next to him was empty, and he could look away and avoid eye contact with Calvin.

Insistent, the youngster again asked, "Are you writing a murder mystery? My mom reads those a lot."

Maurice jotted down another short note that read, "Calvin is on the plane with me and is looking for adventure too." He handed it to Calvin.

The boy grabbed it. He looked at it and then looked back at Maurice with his big brown eyes open wide. "Does this mean I'm gonna be in your book?"

Calvin's conversation with Maurice finally woke up his mother. Maurice leaned over and winked at the boy, as if to confirm that, yes, he may be a character in his book someday. His mother got up and moved Calvin to the middle seat. Maurice explained to her that it was no problem, but he was glad that he might be spared conversation during the entire flight.

That short exchange reminded Maurice how he often thought about adopting a child. Being a single gay man introduced certain challenges to that process, but several of his friends had adopted children and were very content and successful with their fatherhood duties.

"Ladies and gentlemen, the captain has turned off the seat belt sign, and you are free to move about the cabin. We do recommend ..." Her announcement continued, and it was enough to distract little Calvin.

The young female flight attendant who had earlier admonished Maurice to remain in his seat suddenly appeared and asked, "Now, was there something you needed help with, sir?"

Maurice quickly remembered that there was something in his carry-on bag that he wanted to retrieve.

He jumped out of his seat and reached for the overhead compartment. It was a stretch, as he was only five feet eight inches on a good day. He unzipped the front of his carry-on and removed a small bag.

Maurice said to the attendant, "I wanted to give this to you to share with the crew. I know it's a long flight for you guys too." He handed her a clear plastic gift bag of eighty assorted Ghirardelli chocolates.

A bit taken aback, the attendant took a peek at the bag and said, "Oh, my gosh! What a wonderful thing for you to do." She continued, "Wow, I'll definitely let everyone know that Mr. 38B is the generous candy man." She held up the bag to show a nearby crew member.

"My name is Shannon. We'll make sure you have a great flight, sir." She paused, perhaps distracted by Maurice's unusual red hair. His hair sported a fade on the sides and short red curls on the top. Knowing that his unusual crop of hair often drew attention, he frequently would wear a baseball cap to hide the radiant red locks.

She gave him a light tap on the shoulder and continued her inspection down the aisle.

With his chocolate sacrifice to the flying gods now transacted, Maurice tried to settle in and think about the adventure upon which he was about to embark.

He pulled out the airline travel magazine from the seat pocket, opened it, and discreetly placed his pad of paper inside. This way he hoped he could continue writing his notes without drawing attention—Calvin's in particular. He spent a few more minutes writing, filling up at least two pages on his little pad. As he paused for a moment, he happened to look up and noticed Shannon pushing the drink cart down the aisle. He was thirsty and wanted a couple of cocktails to calm his nervous energy.

Shannon pushed the drink cart by his seat and asked, "And what can I offer you today, sir?"

"Shannon, I'd like a screwdriver please." Maurice leaned over to get his wallet out of his back pocket.

Shannon interrupted, "No, no, sir." She placed two small bottles of vodka and orange juice on his tray. "Let me know when you need refills," she offered with a big smile. "It's all on us today."

"Why, thanks. Thanks, very nice of you. It always helps to calm my flying nerves," joked Maurice. He was comforted knowing that he had a "friend" at thirty thousand feet.

He mixed his first drink and took a long sip. With a sigh of relief, he rested his head back on the seat.

After about fifteen minutes, Shannon returned.

"Is everything okay, Mr. Summerlin?"

A bit taken aback by her personalized greeting, he replied, "Yes, just fine, thanks."

"Great. Just contact any of the crew if you need anything. We'll be up all night eating chocolate!" she joked.

Maurice chuckled to himself. "Ha, I would hope they'd be up all night regardless of the chocolate."

Shannon added, "The crew wants to thank you again for the candy. It's not often that someone thinks about us. So, are you traveling on vacation or business?"

While Maurice appreciated her friendly approach, he wasn't in the mood for a lot of conversation.

"Well, it's a special trip I've been planning for a very long time. Vacation, I guess. I did a junior year abroad, and we're having an informal reunion."

"It sounds like an exciting trip," she added. "Well"—she always started her sentences the same way—"Mr. Summerlin, here's another bottle of liquid courage for you." She gently laid it on his lap to avoid attracting the attention of other passengers.

The exchange caught the attention of Calvin.

Leaning around his mother, he yelled, "Hey, mister, did she ask to see your notes? My teacher always wants to see what I'm doodling."

"No, she was just checking on something." Maurice chuckled.

The crew was quick in getting the dinner service underway, and in no time it seemed they were collecting the trays and making a final round of cocktails before darkening the cabin for those wanting to sleep.

Maurice was listening to recorded music on his earphones when a male crew member came by and brought him two bottles of vodka and more orange juice.

Taking off his headphones, Maurice said, "Hey, thanks, man. You guys are trying to get me loaded, huh?"

The male attendant had jet-black hair that was stylishly slicked back. He said with a slight accent, "Well, sir, we all appreciate the chocolates you brought. Do you drink wine?" His name badge said, "R. Cervantes."

"Why, yes, I like wine very much." Maurice cocked his head, wondering why he would ask.

"Well, to show our appreciation, I want to give you a bottle of one of my favorite white wines. We serve it in first class. I hope you enjoy it." The attendant handed Maurice the bottle that he had been hiding behind his back.

As he reached to take the bottle, Maurice noticed the well-manicured hands of the male attendant—a contrast, he thought, to his own thick, hairy forearms and rough hands. Maurice had been a college wrestler for several years, and those arms came in handy during many a match.

"Why, thank you so much. That's very nice of you guys." Maurice noticed that the attendant maintained eye contact throughout their conversation. He wasn't quite sure if the man's dark-brown eyes were being seductive or if the vodka was making him self-conscious. The attendant replied, "Well, Mr. Summerlin, if there's anything else we can do for you the rest of the flight, please let us know."

Maurice thought he saw him wink, but he didn't trust his own observation skills, having just finished his third drink.

Maurice sensed the attendant was interested in continuing their conversation, but he left it at that. It was too early to complicate his vacation. He was somewhat surprised at the interest that one little bag of chocolates had created. *I guess the world is starved for a little common courtesy and kindness,* he thought.

Moments later the crew turned out the lights in the cabin. Most passengers opted to get a little sleep before the long day of jet lag that lay ahead.

Maurice was the exception. He kept his overhead light on so he could continue to write. As he looked down the aisle he saw a single overhead light. He was struck how it illuminated the white hair on the lady several rows ahead. He then imagined how the light above him was probably making his hair appear to be on fire. He reached into his bag to get his cap and covered up his flaming red locks.

Maurice listened to his music and jotted down notes from time to time. It usually was a simple observation about another passenger, like the elderly lady traveling alone, or the two young women together who were constantly giggling, or the two men two rows up and across the aisle who slept with their heads resting against one another. He drifted into his daydream mode and started to wonder about the other passengers on his flight. Were they going or coming? Were they as nervous as he was about venturing away from home, or were they courageous travelers willing to risk leaving the comfort of their homes for a chance to visit new and unusual destinations? Was this just a routine nonevent in their lives or a fulfillment of a dream they once had? He conjured up scenarios of international adventure, exploration, and discovery.

Glancing out the window, Maurice could see snow-covered mountain peaks glistening in the moonlight. All that was familiar had faded. He had no idea what lay ahead of him, though he figured a two-week vacation to a once-familiar Granada would be a relatively safe excursion for his first trip alone. After all, he had reviewed his itinerary and confirmed his reservation several times before leaving. What he was about to learn, however, was that a seasoned traveler always expects the unexpected.

The flight was uneventful. Most passengers either slept or watched the movies. Fortunately for Maurice, Calvin had been focused on the cops and mobsters shooting it out on the video screen in the seatback in front of him.

Maurice drifted off occasionally but tried to stay awake, intent not to waste a minute of his fantasy trip. He was afraid he might miss something that could inspire an important note that he could add to his collection. His challenge was to synthesize pages and pages of notes into a cohesive story. Writing that first chapter was like standing at the end of a diving board, waiting to take the plunge for the first time.

After dozing for a few minutes, he was awakened by the sensation of something dropping in his lap. As he sat up in his seat, several small vodka bottles rattled in his lap. The crew had renewed his medicinal supplies while his was napping.

As he looked up he saw Shannon, the flight attendant, standing over him.

"One more drink for our friend before we arrive?" she asked.

Maurice replied, "Okay, thanks. I just hope I can walk off the plane unassisted!"

She laughed. "Oh, we can assist with that as well!"

"I guess I fell asleep," confessed Maurice.

"And I guess I'm like that nurse who wakes you up to give you a sleeping pill," Shannon joked.

Maurice struggled to open one of the tiny vodka bottles. His big hands seemed to slip while trying to grasp the small cap. Knowing Shannon was watching, he joked, "I know I'm not that drunk. Man, are you guys trying to trick me here?"

"C'mon, with those strong hands this should be a piece of cake," Shannon replied playfully.

Maurice fumbled with the small cap for another minute. She grabbed it out of his hand and whispered, "Here, let a dyke do it."

Maurice was stunned at first. He made eye contact with Shannon, and they both burst out laughing.

"Is arm wrestling next?" challenged Maurice.

"Nah, I think I'll leave the big stuff to the hairy strong man."

Leaning over him, she whispered in a softer tone, "I saw the rainbow pen you've been writing with and figured I'd be safe going there."

Looking at her with a sheepish smile, Maurice added, "Yes, you were."

Maurice was tickled by the playful exchange with Shannon, but he soon realized Calvin again was peeking around his mother. He was curious about the flight attendant's friendly interaction with him.

Fortunately, the announcement that breakfast would soon be served caught Calvin's attention.

Maurice was able to finish his morning cocktail but was afraid to open the other two bottles that he had accumulated through the night. Hoping to avoid stumbling off the plane, he stuffed them in his personal bag that was beneath the seat. It was a stylish leather satchel in the shape of an old mailbag that he had bought just for this trip. He was careful not to scratch the smooth leather when he put it back under the seat.

It wasn't long after they cleared the breakfast trays that the seat belt sign came on and the captain announced that they would be preparing to land in thirty-five minutes.

Everyone was quiet as they disembarked from the plane, moving unusually slow as they shook off the stiffness from the long flight. As Maurice walked up the ramp to the terminal, he felt a tug on his jacket. It was little Calvin.

"Hey, mister, don't forget me in your book. And say nice things about me. I wanna be a good guy."

Maurice patted his little shoulder and said, "Don't worry, pal. I got you covered."

"I'm going to be in his book, Mom!" exclaimed Calvin.

Calvin's mother nodded and thanked Maurice for being so patient with her little boy.

Maurice was amused that this little exchange may have led the little boy to fantasize that he could be a superhero in a book someday.

The check through customs and immigration was fast, and Maurice's luggage was already spilling out on the baggage carousel when he arrived at the claim area.

He paused for a moment. For the first time since he left, he became aware of the unfamiliar noises around him—people talking, luggage moving, and public announcements in several languages. After savoring the moment, he grabbed his one large suitcase. It too was new and didn't yet show the battle scars of the adventurous traveler.

Knowing he'd be tired from the long travel day, he had planned to rest the night in Madrid and rent a car first thing in the morning. After he gathered his luggage, he hailed a cab for his hotel. He had booked a room on the opposite side of town from the airport, near the train station. There was a rental car office there. Weeks before his trip, he studied maps of Madrid and determined he could avoid a harrowing drive through central Madrid if he rented a car on the outskirts of the city. The train station was on the far south side of the city, close to the major highway that headed in the direction of Andalucia and eventually to Granada.

After settling in his small hotel room, Maurice decided to go out for a walk. He wasn't really hungry, as his system was still confused by the jet lag, but he had read that it was best to try to stay up and resist the temptation to take a nap.

As he walked out of his hotel, it didn't take long for the smells of a foreign city to ignite his curiosity. Exhaust from all the motor scooters competed with the smell of food from street vendors.

After a couple of hours of exploring the side streets surrounding the hotel, Maurice walked into a little café he had passed earlier. He thought a beer would be a good way to end his travel day before returning to the hotel for the evening.

The café was small, with several little tables and a circular bar with six or seven stools. The radio was playing old American pop hits. He sat down at the bar and ordered a beer. He was pleased that his Spanish flowed so effortlessly. There were two guys sitting a few stools away on either side of him. One of them looked like a foreigner, an observation that was confirmed when he heard him struggle in Spanish to order another drink.

Having made eye contact with Maurice, the man on his right turned and said, "Hello, chap, where are you from?" The man appeared to be in his mid-forties. He was attractive in a rugged way, his faced creased with lines that were a testament to an active life. "You don't look like a local." He was staring at Maurice's bright-red hair as he spoke.

Maurice was caught off guard by his direct inquiry. "Uh, I'm from the states—Las Vegas, to be exact. How about you?" He twirled his red curls with his finger as he spoke. It was a nervous habit that surfaced whenever he felt uncomfortable or was in an awkward situation. He developed the tic as a child, but as he grew older he became more self-conscious of his little idiosyncrasy. He felt his red hair drew enough attention as it was. As soon as he realized what he was doing, he pulled his hand down to his lap.

The man smiled at Maurice and replied, "I'm from London. I'm on my way back from Andalucia. Are you visiting here in Madrid?"

Maurice answered, "Actually, I'm driving to Andalucia in the morning. I'm going to spend a couple of weeks visiting in Granada."

"Granada is a spectacular place. I've been to most parts of Spain, but it's hard to beat the beauty of the Alhambra." The man took a sip from his stein of beer.

Maurice leaned closer, as the stranger spoke in a thick British accent to which he wasn't accustomed.

The man continued, "Yeah, I'm taking the train up north today."

Maurice asked, "Vacation?"

The Brit replied, "No, just exploring. I'm going to check out the northern Spanish coast for a while. I might settle down there for a couple of months. I dabble in painting—watercolors usually. Other than that I have no real plans. I'm Clifford, by the way."

"Nice to meet you. I'm Maurice. What do you do? I mean, do you work?"

As soon as he spoke, Maurice felt stupid asking him about his work. It was pretty clear from his bohemian dress and old duffel bag that he was not a businessman.

"No, like I said, I paint a little, but I can't make much of a living doing that. I've thought about teaching English—you know, ESL—in one of the small cities on the coast. There are a lot of small language schools that will hire you for a few months to teach."

Not sure how to respond, Maurice said, "Cool, I wish you luck."

Clifford replied, "Well, mate, life's too short to sit in one place too long."

Hesitant at first to get too personal, Maurice asked, "How long have you been traveling?"

"I've been in Spain for nearly a year. I sold my flat in London, along with most of my belongings. After my marriage fell apart I realized I had deferred a lot of things that I wanted to see and do. Don't know if you're married, mate, but if you are, don't stop being you."

"Well, sorry about that … but I mean … it's great you're out doing what you want now," Maurice said awkwardly.

Clifford replied, "I felt guilty at first—you know, all my friends were responsible and had good jobs. They all told me I was crazy. But for now I know I need to keep moving. That's what's best for me. In fact, a while back I had a great experience down in Andalucia that helped to validate and legitimize what I'm doing. Wanderlust, I guess you could call it."

Maurice was struck by Clifford's free spirit and seeming lack of concern about relocating somewhere he had never been—and without a job, no less. He thought, *And here I am fretting about a two-week vacation away from home. I don't know if I'd ever have the courage to give it all up someday like Clifford and dare to try something completely new.*

Clifford looked at his watch. "Oops, gotta run and catch my train." He took a final swig of his beer and left some change on the bar.

"I wish you a good trip … uh, Maurice, right? And enjoy Granada!" He reached down and swung a large duffel bag over his shoulder.

As he left, Maurice looked at all the stains and tiny tears in the bag. He imagined all the places where that poor bag had been and the stories contained within it. The fantasy of adventure was like an opiate to him, even though he had never taken the initiative to plan one of his own.

Clifford took off so fast that Maurice didn't have a chance to ask him what the experience was that validated his need to live the loose and free life—wanderlust, as he called it. Their chance encounter was brief, but the daydreams ignited by their short conversation stayed with Maurice the rest of the evening.

Maurice woke up early and helped himself to the continental breakfast set up in the hotel lobby. Other than an elderly lady having coffee at the corner table, the hotel was quiet. The breakfast was simple: coffee, orange juice, some mixed rolls and marmalade, and fruit. He ate quickly, as he was excited to start the long drive south. The intensity of the blue sky was broken by an occasional fluffy white cloud. A dry, warm breeze from the south was welcoming. The good traveling weather was one less thing for him to worry about.

The train station was less than a block from the hotel. As he walked across the street with his suitcase in tow, he saw the rental car sign pointing toward the back of the train station. Maurice found the short walk a challenge, as he had to pull his suitcase through crowds of anxious commuters rushing for their respective trains.

Once at the rental car counter, he was relieved to find his reservation in order. After a quick check-in, he located his car, loaded his suitcase in the back, and placed his maps in the front seat, where he could refer to them while driving. He had brought a few bottles of water and some protein bars for the trip as well, and set them in the console next to him.

With the mirrors and driver's seat adjusted, he sat motionless for a moment. After taking a deep breath, a few beads of sweat formed on his forehead. He said to himself, "Well, Maurice, this is what you have wanted for a long time. You're here now. Make the most of it."

He had rewarded himself with a brief moment of self-congratulations for having come this far, breaking the pull of gravity that kept him close to home. He laughed at himself, hoping there was no one nearby watching him talk to the dashboard. Before he shut the door, he happened to look up. Above him was a large billboard with a photo of a young couple zip-lining over a junglelike canopy. Roughly translated, the caption read, "Explore your limits. Join Adventurers' Club!"

It would have been no surprise to Maurice's friends that he had studied the details of the Spanish roadmap and was already familiar with the main highway route that would take him south from Madrid. He would cross the legendary land of La Mancha and go on to the southern-most of Spain's provinces, Andalucia. There he would arrive at his final destination, the Moorish city of Granada. It was early morning, and while still tired from the previous day's flight, he figured he could travel at a leisurely pace and still arrive before nightfall. He estimated the drive would take about six hours. Hoping to avoid drawing unnecessary attention to himself, he put on his blue Cubs hat, knowing that his exposed red curls would act like a beacon to the curious. He chuckled to himself, as he also knew that this particular hat would garner him no words of sympathy as it would in the states.

As he drove away from the train station to maneuver onto the main highway, he realized he was going to have to adjust quickly to the unfamiliar road signs. He muttered, "Damn, I should have studied these signs before I left." While most signs were obvious, there were some that left him guessing. He noted these on the writing pad he placed conveniently on the passenger seat. He would look them up at his next stop.

Watching the lively metropolis of Madrid disappear in his rear-view mirror, he recalled what a great city it was, but it wasn't the energy he was looking for on this trip. He hoped that Granada, a city of only 175,000 people compared to Madrid's five million, would provide a more reflective environment in which he could forget about the predictable life he left behind, if even for just two weeks.

He often had fantasized about exploring on his own, trying things he hadn't done before, eating things he hadn't tasted before, and meeting people who had different outlooks on life, but he knew this also would be his greatest challenge. He wanted to absorb the spirit of his surroundings with the hope that it would somehow inspire him to write something other than those boring business pieces.

As he got farther from Madrid, the highway became surprisingly free of traffic. The four-lane highway narrowed to two lanes. He looked upon vast stretches of rolling hills with little vegetation and only occasional adobe farm buildings with red-tiled roofs to remind him of civilization. He stared at the unfamiliar landscape ahead of him, often coming to the terrifying realization that he didn't remember driving the previous ten minutes. Maurice had perfected the art of daydreaming and used to joke that if he could get paid for it, he'd be one of the wealthiest men on the planet.

Back home he would take the train from the West Coast back east when visiting family. Coworkers and friends would kid him that he was old-fashioned and advised that he should fly instead. They would argue that they would lose their minds sitting on a train for two and a half days. He'd ignore their comments because he knew once he boarded the train and settled into his little sleeper compartment, he'd be entering a different world. He could stare out his window for hours, watching the passing landscape, even waking up at night to look out the window and watch as the moon appeared to move along with the train as they sped through mountain passes, over rivers, and across the plains.

Not more than an hour out of Madrid, he approached the area known as La Mancha. He glanced toward the horizon and noticed several of the iconic windmills on a distant hillside. These historic structures were immortalized in Cervantes's *Don Quixote*. Maurice stared at them, trying to imagine how the quixotic and delusional hero fought them, believing they were enemy soldiers. Over two hundred years old, the sense of history symbolized by these windmills was particularly striking to Maurice, who was from Las Vegas, where "old" was defined as "it hadn't been rained on in nine months."

Unlike the delusional Don Quixote in his battles with his antagonistic windmills, Maurice faced his own internal battle against a lack of self-confidence and spontaneity. He wondered at what point his own dreams might become real.

As he traveled down the almost empty highway, he stared at the passing landscape, a dry and seemingly empty panorama, a gritty mix of sand and rocks. He'd see an occasional field of olive trees or a small vineyard. There was little sign of life except for an occasional goat herder tending to his valuable family. He wondered how such a robust ancient Spanish empire arose from such a desolate landscape, forgetting for the moment that much of the wealth and treasure were imported from colonies and conquered lands abroad. He also knew that southern Spain—and the province of Andalucia, in particular—had resources and wealth accumulated by centuries of Moorish rule.

Time passed quickly. He already had been on the road for over two hours. He made several short stops for a cup of espresso and pastries. He stopped in one tiny village called *Cinco Casas* (Five Houses). He chuckled out loud. "They must have counted wrong. There are only four." Each house appeared very old with thick fort-like adobe walls and old wooden beams over the window frames and doorways. Many of the red tiles on the roofs were disheveled or missing. The small café accommodated a small bar inside, with several tables outside. The tables outside were crowded, so he sat at the bar inside, where he enjoyed the smell of coffee that filled the small room. The churro, a sticklike fried pastry covered in sugar, brought back memories of the sugary dessert he enjoyed while a student in Granada.

Recalling the advice of his good friend Sheila, he tried to resist the temptation to drive straight through to Granada. In the past he would focus on the destination instead of enjoying the journey. With that in mind, he purposely pulled off to the side of the road to enjoy a panoramic view of the landscape with the windmills standing guard atop a distant hillside.

As he drove farther, the hills grew into small mountains, and he knew he was getting closer to Granada. But the sky was changing even faster than the landscape. The blue sky over the brown plains of La Mancha had been replaced by an ominously dark gray ceiling, which increasingly appeared to be hugging the green and more heavily wooded mountainsides. He cracked open his window to let in the fresh, moist air. It had that sweet damp smell that would often precede a rainstorm.

Within a half hour it started to rain—sporadically at first and then a steady drizzle. Before long the rain became heavy and he had to roll up his window and turn on the windshield wipers. There was little traffic on the highway, but he noticed the few cars coming toward him had turned on their headlights.

In the next fifteen minutes, things changed dramatically. The wind began to buffet the car from side to side, and the veins in his hands stood out as he gripped the steering wheel more tightly. In no time the rain was coming down so hard that it made a roar on the roof of the little rental car.

He slowed down to half his speed. The little windshield wipers were going as fast as they could, but he could barely make out the road ahead of him. It rained like this for another hour. He saw fewer and fewer cars coming toward him, and after a while he couldn't remember when the last one had passed him.

At one point he slowed down to a near stop upon seeing water rushing across the highway from a "wash," or riverbed, that was probably dry most of the year.

He said to himself, "And I thought the rain in Spain fell mainly on the plain!"

He continued slowly making his way over what appeared to be a wooded mountain pass. As he began to descend down the other side, the darkness of the clouds, the sheets of rain, and the mountain shadows obscured the horizon.

He drove for another few minutes, believing that any time he would see a sign for the highway exit that would take him to Granada. Despite being slowed down by the weather, he thought it was still early and he had time to take it slow and easy.

As he rounded a turn, he saw flashing lights on the side of the road. As he got closer, there appeared to be a woman in a blue hooded jacket standing by a car, waving her arms. She was yelling in his direction, but he couldn't hear anything with his windows closed. He slowed down to pull over. He was a little nervous about helping a stranger in a foreign land, but he couldn't ignore coming to aid a lady who appeared to be stranded alone on the highway.

He slowly pulled up behind her car. The lady rushed toward him and motioned for him to back up. He still couldn't understand what she was saying, even with the windows rolled partially down. After backing up about ten yards, he noticed smoke coming from under her hood.

The woman ran up to the passenger side of his car. He opened the door, and she scampered into the passenger seat. Soaking wet, she pulled down the hood from her jacket, exposing the face of a surprisingly older lady with short white hair. He thought it strange that an elderly woman would be traveling alone. Her wrinkled face was drizzled with raindrops. Maurice handed her some napkins from his console. She wiped her face and took a deep breath.

He was about to nervously ask in Spanish what was wrong, but she spoke first.

"Do you speak English, young man?" she inquired, a bit out of breath.

"Why, yes, what happened to your car? Are you okay?" Maurice asked nervously.

"I'm fine, but that cheap piece of engineering is going up in flames, and I wasn't about to join it." Despite the situation, she managed to smile.

"You sound American. Do you live here or just traveling?" Maurice inquired.

"Let's say I'm visiting old friends." She winked.

Maurice didn't want to pry, but he sensed there might be more to her situation than first indicated. He asked, "Where are you headed?"

"Well, I was on a cruise that terminated in Lisbon. I have friends in a little village north of Almería, just about one hundred miles from here, and I thought I'd drive from Lisbon across southern Spain to visit them. It didn't look that far on the map, but I guess I may have bit off more than I could handle. I'm afraid if I don't show up, they'll be worried."

Maurice sat listening, not sure how to respond or what to do.

"My name is Claire, by the way. What's your name?

"I'm Maurice. I was—"

Claire interrupted before he could finish. "Where are you going?"

A bit taken aback by her forward nature, Maurice continued, "Well, I'm on my way to Granada to visit the university where I went to school many years ago."

"How nice, young man. Granada is a very special place, at least to me. There's a deep spirituality there. It's hard to describe. Maybe it comes from its ancient Moorish legacy."

Claire seemed to ignore the fact that her car was on fire. She asked, "Are you going to visit friends?"

"I don't suppose too many of my friends are still there. I'm really out to ..." He paused for a second, unsure how much he should share with her. "I think I just want to take in the experience again ... and hopefully view things from a new perspective now that I'm all grown up." He chuckled, thinking he was being clever and cute.

Trying to address the smoke coming from her car, Maurice suggested, "I think we should try to call—"

Claire interrupted, still not appearing to be concerned about her car. "We never grow up. We should always remain a bit restless, just enough to keep us interested, alert, and in search of whatever it is that we're drawn to. It doesn't sound like you're all that sure of why you're here. But that's okay. You'll find out. That's the fun of discovery."

Claire seemed to be drifting into a philosophical space. Maurice found himself thinking how unlike him it was to be sitting in a car with a stranded stranger, having such a personal and what seemed at the time irrelevant conversation.

He wasn't distracted from the fact that it was still pouring outside and full darkness had all but arrived.

Anxious to continue on his drive, he interrupted Claire. "Well, Claire, I'm not sure what to do. I have hotel reservations in Granada and I'd be happy to take you there. I'm sure you can straighten out your car situation and contact your friends."

Claire sat still, looking out the side window. The momentary silence gave Maurice pause for concern.

"Maurice," Claire started to say, "I have a request ... well, I guess it's more of a proposal."

A tingle went up Maurice's spine as he straightened up in anticipation of what his gray-haired passenger was about to propose.

"Yes?" He twirled his fingers in his hair nervously.

"I'd like you to take me to San Felipe, the village where my friends live. I'll pay you for your time and gas. You could stay the night and drive back to Granada in the morning. It's only a few hours away and—"

Maurice tried to respond, "Well, I'm not sure that's—"

Claire interrupted him again. "Maurice, you did say you wanted to experience things from a new perspective, right? I think a young man like you would like my little village."

He thought, *Yes, I did say that. My gosh, she sounds like my therapist.*

Before he could even think of responding, she continued, "I really think you will enjoy this little side trip. And my friends are *very special.*" She placed extra emphasis on "very special."

"Well, it's still early. I guess I could drive you there. Hopefully, the weather will clear up and I can make the trip back to Granada later tonight."

Claire reached over and squeezed his forearm. "Thanks, sweetie. My goodness … big strong arms!"

Maurice shook his head, hiding a smile. He nervously laughed to himself. *I'm being hustled by a little old lady.*

"Are you sure you know the way from here?" Maurice asked.

Claire chuckled. "Not all of us who wander are lost, my friend. And I say that in the broadest sense."

Maurice thought for a moment about the full meaning of what his newly acquired traveling companion just said.

Claire dashed out the door and ran to her car to retrieve a large bag out of her trunk. Maurice started to get out to help, but she waved him back in and yelled, "I got this, Maurice. No sense in both of us getting soaked."

Despite the situation and the conditions, Claire seemed delighted to have made a new friend. Maurice was not yet convinced this was an entirely good idea, but something told him to go with it.

He thought, *This was part of the experience I wanted … to meet people … and I guess one can't always pick and choose the moment.*

"Where are you from again?" she asked.

Maurice had never really said, but he answered, "Las Vegas."

Claire acknowledged with a sigh, "Ah, so you're a gambler," she joked, "… with money or in life?"

"Well, I don't play much in the casinos, really, and I'm not much of a risk taker in life either, I guess. This trip is a big deal for me." Maurice surprised himself with his confession.

The rain was still pounding on the roof of the car as they sat parked on the side of the road. Maurice began to wonder where this was leading.

"Why a big deal? Isn't it exciting to be on a new journey for a change?" Claire replied with a challenging tone in her voice.

"Yes, I really am excited. It's just …" Maurice hesitated, trying to think of what he wanted to say.

"Just what?"

"I daydream of adventures all the time but never really follow through with any of them. This time I am. I hope I'm doing the right thing. Too late now to question that, isn't it?" he joked.

Claire commented, "There's nothing you should be fearful of, young man. If it's out of our control, there's no sense in worrying, and if it is in our control, embrace it."

Claire's questioning made Maurice a bit anxious, but he responded, "I guess I'm just nervous being away from all that I love at home, but I know deep inside that it will always be there when I get back."

"Yes. See? You answered your own question. Enjoy the journey, Maurice. When you learn to let go, you'll feel a tingling inside. I tingle all the time in my old age." Claire giggled loudly and gave Maurice a little poke in his side.

She added, "I hope I don't sound like a fortune cookie dispensing all this advice. I paid dearly for my wisdom and just want to share it with you."

Maurice turned to Claire, trying to convey his appreciation with a nod and a smile. But given the pounding rain on the roof and his preoccupation with the sudden change of itinerary, he wasn't able to process everything she was saying.

"So you'll have to show me the route. I have no idea where we're going now." Maurice pulled out onto the highway. He clenched the steering wheel firmly, as the rain and wind were still a problem and the road curved sharply as they made switchbacks down the mountain pass.

"No problem. I know this route well. I've made this trip many times," Claire said with confidence.

"Did you live here before?" Maurice asked.

"Live, no, but my husband brought me here once. He was a jazz musician. A bandmate of his was from here and invited us to a jazz festival. Since the death of my husband, I've returned every year for a couple of weeks to renew my vows, so to speak."

"Renew your vows? I don't understand." Maurice wanted to look at her but had to keep his eyes on the road.

"I mean vows in the personal sense. I vow to keep an active and open mind. I vow to keep busy exploring and searching for experiences that make me tingle inside." Claire wiggled in her seat, imitating a tingling sensation.

Maurice shook his head and smiled.

She continued, "You know, imagination can alter our perceptions of things, and eventually our attitudes. I come here to be with my friends who have mastered what I call 'open soul surgery.'"

Maurice remained silent and just listened. Still a bit unsure who this lady was sitting next to him, he was finding himself being drawn to her, wanting to understand the journey she was on.

Claire continued, "I'm an old woman now. Not that the age of our bodies has to match that of our mind and our heart. It's just that I know I'm at the crossroads of life's last episode, and I want to make the most of it."

Maurice relaxed his firm grip on the steering wheel for the first time.

He added, "I must say, you are not the typical hitchhiker I would have expected to pick up." The rain was easing up, and he was beginning to feel more comfortable with Claire as his passenger.

Claire gently tapped his knee with her delicate hand and said, "You need to relax, young man. There are so many avenues open to you. Caution is good, but I sense you are too busy weighing probabilities against possibilities. Let it all go." She threw her hands up, as if tossing all the fear and restraint into the air.

The weather had improved enough that Maurice decided to stop at a small café. He needed to make a pit stop, and an espresso sounded appealing.

Claire walked over to a small table in the corner. The café was similar to the one Maurice had stopped at earlier. The only other patron was an older man at the bar watching a soccer game on the small TV behind the bar. They both enjoyed their coffee and some toasted bread without saying much. Eager to jot down a myriad of thoughts he had while driving, Maurice pulled out his notepad and started writing. He usually wouldn't write in front of someone, but he didn't want to take the chance of losing his thoughts. Of course, Claire asked him what he was writing.

Maurice didn't want to have to explain too much at this particular moment and just said he was a writer and that he liked to keep notes. Before Claire could ask any questions, he got up to use the men's room, and when he came back Claire had paid the bill and was waiting by the door.

They drove for another twenty minutes. Claire was focused on reading the road signs. She cautioned Maurice, "Slow down, dear. I think we're getting close to town."

There was a weathered sign ahead pointing to the right that said "S n Feli ." Several of the letters were completely missing.

"That's it. We're almost there. It's a tiny place, so slow down or we'll pass right through it without you knowing it." She had a big smile on her face. "Maurice, this is San Felipe. The town has only 175 permanent residents, but it's a well-known fishing village, and nearby are some of the best beaches in Spain, if not the entire Mediterranean."

Claire directed Maurice into town and down a narrow street. She motioned for him to pull in front of a well-lit little shop with a sign that read, "Pastelería Fina."

Claire quickly got out of the car and motioned for Maurice to follow her.

The rain had stopped, but everything was wet and the gurgling sound of the water still running down the street from the recent showers broke the silence of the evening. The air was heavy but pleasant, thick with a sweet fragrance that Maurice didn't recognize. He held his head up to take a big breath.

"That's jasmine you smell, dear. Isn't it delirious?" Claire stood and took a deep breath too.

Maurice was surprised at the intensity of the scent that filled the air. Without thinking he said, "Yes, it's delicious."

"Deliriously delicious then!" Claire replied. She was clearly amused by Maurice's comment.

"We'll stay here. My friend Fina owns the pastry shop. I'm sure we can spend the night with her and go up to the hill in the morning and meet my friends."

Maurice tensed up. With eyes squinting he stared downward at the little Ms. Claire and politely protested, "Claire, I have a hotel reservation and should head back tonight. The rain stopped and—"

Claire, as usual, interrupted. "Maurice, it'll be okay. I'll have Fina contact the hotel for you and let them know the storm has delayed your arrival for a day or two." For good measure she added, "It's too dangerous to go back on the highway now."

Before he could say another word, she reached and grabbed his hand. "Let's go in and meet Fina. We'll talk more inside."

The town was quiet, as everyone had retreated inside during the unusual but welcome rain. The old wrought iron lights hanging on the front of each building cast a warm glow in the mistiness of the evening. Their reflections sparkled on the wet cobblestones of the narrow streets.

Fina's shop was in an old two-story building. A small blue awning hung over the entrance. Colorful geraniums on the iron balconies above the entrance partially obscured tall wooden shutters. Maurice paused and looked up at what was an iconic Spanish scene.

Claire said, "You're in Spain now, Maurice. Enjoy all it has to offer." Claire squeezed his hand, which completely enveloped her tiny fingers.

Wearing their fatigue like old coats, they walked up to the door. Claire rang a little bell by the entrance, but Fina had already heard them pull up and was starting to open the door. Fina was a short, full-figured lady of middle age, with black hair pulled back into a bun. She wore no makeup, but her pleasantly young-looking face didn't demand it either.

"*Mi cielo!*" announced Fina as she embraced Claire. "Welcome back!" Fina gave a curious glance at Claire's young companion.

Claire responded, "*Hola*, Fina, it is so good to see you again. I almost didn't make it except for the help of this gallant young man."

Maurice nodded, taking off his baseball cap. His red curls sprung from beneath his cap. He heard Fina utter, "Oh my."

Maurice was accustomed to this reaction.

Fina warmly greeted him, "Welcome to our little village."

Maurice replied, "It's very nice to meet you. I'm supposed to be in Granada tonight, but I saw Claire stranded on the highway and—"

"I know, *hijo,* you were so nice to stop and help her," Fina explained. She affectionately called Maurice *hijo,* or son.

Maurice scratched his head and thought to himself, *My goodness, does everyone complete my sentences? And how does Fina know that I picked up Claire on the highway?*

Fina continued, "Claire called me from the road and told me you guys were on your way. Come sit down, I have some warm soup and bread for you." Fina spoke with a heavy Spanish accent.

Maurice threw a look of "aha" directly at Claire, who bounced her head from side to side with a curious smile, as if to say, "Yeah, busted."

Maurice felt something on the back of his legs. He turned around and was a bit startled to find a big golden retriever sniffing his behind.

Fina interrupted, "Oh, she's okay. That's Sucre. She's an old girl. Very sweet. Been with me for more than twelve years." Fina chuckled. "*Sucre* means 'sweet' in French." She continued, "I've made up beds in both guest rooms, and I put on an extra blanket since it's a bit cool tonight." Fina placed a hot bowl of soup in front of each of them.

The rising steam from the hot broth prompted Maurice to pause and inhale through his nose. A sip confirmed it was chicken, but it had a little spicy bite that was pleasing after his long ride.

"This is awfully nice of you, Fina. I hate to impose. I do need to call my hotel though," Maurice added.

"Oh, don't worry, *hijo.* Leave me the number and I can call for you." Her chubby arms jiggled as she moved her arms and hands while she talked.

Maurice nodded okay, although he was usually compulsive in wanting to follow up on his own details. Giving up control was one of the first demons he had to set free, and Claire seemed to recognize this.

Claire finished her soup first and walked over to the kitchen to visit with Fina. Maurice could hear them chatter but could not make out the entire conversation. Fina mentioned something about someone named "Julian," and he heard Claire respond, "How terrible!" They continued to chat for a few moments, glancing over to Maurice before giving one another a supportive hug.

They came back to the table, where Maurice was finishing up his soup. He tried to hide his discomfort with having discovered a chicken claw at the bottom of his soup bowl.

Standing behind him, Fina asked, "Did you like the soup, *hijo?*" She placed both of her hands on his shoulders.

"Ah, yes, it was delicious."

Perhaps it was again inevitable, but Fina, still standing behind Maurice, commented, "You know, I had a cousin many years ago who had hair like yours. We called him *Fuego*, for 'fire.' Most believed his hair was a sign of good fortune."

"And did he really have good luck?" asked Maurice.

"Well," explained Fina, her hands tapping Maurice's shoulders, "sort of. One day as he was riding his horse around his property, the animal got spooked and took off through the woods. Fuego got knocked off by a low tree limb and never regained consciousness."

"Good grief, that sounds more like bad luck to me." Maurice twirled his fingers nervously through his red curls while he spoke.

Fina continued, "Well, unfortunately for Fuego, yes, but as it turned out, when the townspeople started preparing to build their park on the land that he donated, they discovered some old ruins. The government determined it was an ancient site where the Moors had built a mosque in the twelfth century. The Ministry of Archaeology paid the town dearly to purchase and preserve the site."

Claire chuckled. "I guess the town drew the lucky straw.

Let's hope there's some good fortune in those fiery curls of yours, Maurice!"

Claire hesitated and then added, "I have a feeling there will be."

Maurice looked at her and joked, "Claire, you're scaring me!"

Fina laughed and said, "We can chat more in the morning. I know you both must be tired from the drive. Let me show you to your rooms."

The two travelers followed Fina up the stairs to their rooms.

As Maurice entered his room, Sucre came scurrying up the stairs as fast as a twelve-year-old dog could scurry and followed him in to his room.

Fina called, "Sucre, come here and leave that man alone."

Sucre had jumped on Maurice's bed and lay there, looking at him.

Fina, with her hands cradling her round face, said, "Oh my, she normally doesn't take to strangers so quickly." Clearly surprised, she walked into the room and led Sucre back out to the hall.

Maurice said, "That's okay. I used to have a big dog at home who slept with me."

"Well, you need your rest. You and Sucre have a lot of time to get acquainted."

At that moment Claire reached for Maurice and gave him a big hug. Even though Maurice was not a tall man, she was a short little thing and her head rested easily on Maurice's chest.

She looked up at him and said, "Thank you for everything, Maurice. You are a good person, and I think there are good things in store for you."

Maurice gave her a squeeze, saying, "You're more than welcome, Claire."

Claire walked down the hall to her room.

Maurice closed his door and let out a big sigh. The room was cozy and simply furnished with a bed and small dresser. He could smell the fresh air coming through the wooden shutters that were slightly ajar.

His thoughts hung for a moment on some of the comments made that evening, such as "You and Sucre have a lot of time to get acquainted," "Good things will happen to you," and "You'll like my friends up on the hill."

He normally would have obsessed about all the references that implied a longer visit, but he was exhausted. The bed looked warm and comfortable. It wasn't long before his daydreams succumbed to a deep sleep.

Maurice woke up early. The first light of the day had barely broken through the sheer drapes covering the tall shutter doors on his balcony. When he opened the shutters, he immediately smelled the same sweet fresh air that he had noticed when they arrived the night before. The balcony was just wide enough to step outside. The narrow street lined with whitewashed buildings was quiet except for the muffled echoes of two older men talking in the corner. A dog was walking down the street, moving slowly but intently, as if he had a particular place where he needed to be. Maurice couldn't see the ocean from where he was standing, but there was a salty dampness in the air that led him to believe it wasn't far away.

He stood on the balcony for quite a long time before he decided he'd better get cleaned up.

After he showered and got dressed, he sat on the bed, contemplating his plans for completing his trip to Granada. Claire had mentioned more than once about "going up the hill to meet her special friends." He was curious and figured he had nothing to lose at this point by going up there with her. He calculated that he had all day to make the short drive back to Granada.

As he was about to leave his room, he heard a whimpering sound outside his door. As soon as he opened the door, Sucre bounded in and jumped on his bed. She sat looking at Maurice, as if she was inviting him to sit next to her. He did just that, and Sucre instantly put her head in Maurice's lap.

"Guess you guys are best buddies already," said Fina as she poked her head into the room. "I'm impressed that Sucre has taken a liking to you so quickly."

"She's a sweetie, that's for sure," replied Maurice as he rubbed Sucre's furry neck.

Claire appeared right behind Fina and added, "Maurice, dear, looks like you're up for the day. Why don't you come down and join us for coffee and toast."

"Sure will. I'll be right down. I need to check with my hotel in Granada first."

Claire immediately responded, "Not necessary. Fina already called."

Despite Claire's reassurances, Maurice was still unclear what the status of his reservation was. "Are they holding the room for me? Did they say it was okay?"

Without exactly answering his question, Fina responded, "Everything is okay, *hijo*. Not to worry."

As hard as it was for Maurice to let go, he took a leap of faith and assumed that Fina and Claire had taken care of things as they had promised.

They all went downstairs, Sucre following closely behind Maurice. On the way down the stairs, Maurice heard the cries of a little baby.

"Oh," he said with a little surprise on his face, "you have a child, Fina?"

Fina and Claire, already at the bottom of the stairs, glanced at each other quickly. Hesitating for a second, Fina answered, "Yes, an adorable little boy."

They hurried out to the kitchen without saying more. Maurice thought their dismissal of the conversation was a bit odd, but he was preoccupied with his own schedule for the day, so he quickly followed them into the kitchen.

Fina's house had an outdoor terrace just off the kitchen. The floor was covered in tiles whose cracks gave away their age. The walls were covered with pots of blooming geraniums, each pot hanging securely from an iron holder attached at different levels on the wall. In the corner, a purple bougainvillea spilled over the wall, leaving many of its fallen petals to create a mottled carpet of color on the beige tile floor.

They sat at a small square table with a little bowl of sugar sitting in the middle. Fina brought out a tray with three small cups of coffee.

"This is *café con leche*. I hope that's okay. If you don't like a lot of milk, I can make you an espresso?"

"No, this is great, thanks. I love the coffee here. It has a little kick compared to what we're used to back in the states." Maurice actually preferred the espresso, but he didn't want Fina to go to any more trouble.

Fina brought out a tray of toast, butter, and marmalade and placed it in the center of the table. "I made the pear marmalade myself. I hope you like it." Fina clearly enjoyed having guests come by to visit.

They sipped their coffee for a few minutes. While Maurice buttered his toast, Claire broke the silence.

"So, Maurice, I remember you said you were a writer. Novels, poems, short stories?" Claire had her elbows on the table, and she was looking directly at Maurice.

Maurice was caught a little off guard but wasn't surprised that she remembered his mentioning that he was a writer. "Yes, I am ... sorta ... I mean yes. I write feature articles for a local business magazine … more human interest stories like … uh …" He hesitated, as he rarely ever had to explain to anyone what he did for a living. He continued, "Mostly articles about programs in the local university for continuing education or topics like solar energy. Things that future businesses might want to know before considering relocating their businesses to Las Vegas."

Claire said, "Well, that's very interesting, although from your hesitation I'm not sure that you're very excited about your work."

No one had ever questioned or analyzed Maurice in that way before. While such inquires normally would have been off-putting to Maurice, there was an authenticity in Claire's comments that made him feel more comfortable engaging her.

"Truth is," Maurice confessed as he pulled on some of his red curls, "I'm not thrilled with it. It pays the bills, but I really want to write something meaningful—at least meaningful to me. I want to write a novel and have it published."

Claire nodded and raised her hands in front of her, as if to say, "Hallelujah." "That's it, Maurice. You've got your destination. Now let your instincts and a little fate help to guide you in your pursuit."

Claire added, "Well, Mr. Maurice, are you ready to continue your journey today?"

"I'm not sure what you mean by 'journey,' but you did mention going up the hill to meet your friends. Is that what you're referring to?" Maurice knew what she meant, but he was hoping she would elaborate more about any ulterior motives that she and Fina may have had.

"Yes." Claire continued, "But first I want to tell you a little about my friends and the place they have up the hill. It's a very special place, as are they, and you need to understand a bit of the background of how this all came about. Do you want another coffee? This may take a little while." She smiled and appeared to settle herself in for a long conversation.

"Sure," replied Maurice. He tried to get comfortable, but the anxiety that started to slowly sweep through his body made him fidget in his chair. Sucre walked up and sat next to him. He rested his hand on her furry head, which helped him to relax.

Claire began her story.

"About seven years ago, a young professor from a university not too far away bought the property up on the hill. I think he intended someday to raise a family there and perhaps retire early and write. The property was in terrible condition, but he was excited about restoring it. Many years ago it was a retreat for a group of nuns from a monastery in Granada.

"The professor—Julian is his name—was quite different from most of the townspeople. His complexion was dark, and he had black hair."

Claire took a sip of her coffee. Maurice stroked Sucre as he listened.

Claire continued, "Despite his foreign appearance, he spoke very good Spanish and English. He was originally from Morocco and was a respected scholar both there and in Granada."

Fina injected, "He did have a slight accent though, so we knew that neither Spanish nor English was his native language. It was obvious he was not from here."

Claire added, "And you know how a small isolated town can feel about a stranger that looks and sounds different from them. Anyway, I should let Fina continue since she was the one who first met him."

Fina resumed the story. "Yes, well, Julian was a very nice young man, and whenever he came down to the village for supplies he made a point to stop and buy bread and pastries from me. He loved to chat. I think he stopped more for that than the pastries. Over time we became very good friends, and occasionally I'd invite him over for dinner."

While Fina recounted her story, Sucre had rested her head on Maurice's lap. Maurice noticed Fina's approving smile.

She said, "Like you, *hijo*, Sucre took to Julian as if he were her master. Sometimes she'd spend the entire day with him up on the hill. I knew there was something special about Julian. Like I said, Sucre is a good judge of people, and I trust her instincts.

"Now, I also have a sister in town—her name is Elena. She is not really well in the head, as we say. She has a history of emotional problems, and many of the townspeople had become afraid of her because of the occasional tirades she would have—throwing flowerpots, yelling in the middle of the town plaza, and even taking some of my pastries and squishing them on the storefront windows."

Fina paused to laugh at the thought of those pastries on their windows.

"Sometimes Elena would walk to the ocean and wade out until she couldn't touch the bottom. She couldn't swim and would start screaming. I've been lucky that there was always someone nearby willing to rescue her. This small village easily imagined the worst—that Elena could be insane or even that she could be possessed. Some of the residents of San Felipe even threatened us and demanded we both leave town."

Fina explained that, before her parents passed away, she had been going to the University of Valencia but had to quit school to take care of her sister. She took over her parents' bakery to make ends meet.

"Well, as time went on, Julian had become acquainted with Elena and occasionally invited her up to his property. It wasn't a romantic attraction, but I think he felt sorry for her and hoped he could help improve her disposition. For some reason Elena became attached to Julian, and he became one of the few people she would trust. She loved to watch him do his chores, and I guess she, in turn, provided him some company."

Fina added that they would talk and joke with each other. As Julian spent more time with Elena, he would give her routine tasks to do. Fina noticed that her episodes of emotional outbursts became fewer.

Fina paused for a moment and took a bite of her toast and a sip of coffee.

"Whenever Elena started to feel depressed or out of sorts, she knew to come to Julian. He could not always alter her disposition, but he certainly provided her refuge and comfort, something that no one previously had been able to do, including me."

Maurice was listening so intently that his coffee had cooled off. Claire went to the kitchen to reheat it.

Fina explained that Julian would take Elena to Almería, the largest nearby city, where he was able to get her medication that minimized her episodes. None of this went unnoticed by the people in our little village. While some suspicion about Julian lingered, they remained in awe of his capacity to change Elena into what they perceived as a new person. Some claimed it was a miracle.

Claire added, "This legacy has followed Julian ever since."

Fina said, "To bring you up to date, before Julian retired from the university, he married a young lady who was from a place near his hometown in southern Morocco. It's a very troubled area, from what I understand. Anyway, they had a baby, and not long after that, she was murdered. The police never solved the murder, but Julian was sure it had to do with members of her family who did not approve of their marriage."

Claire explained that Julian still lived up the hill, but since he was afraid that his wife's family would try to kidnap his little boy, he asked Fina to help take care of him. She said she had been taking care of the two-year-old since he was a baby.

Fina started to become a little agitated recounting the next part of the story. "Well, Julian was badly beaten a few days ago just outside of town. The *policia* brought him back to my bakery because they knew we were friends. He's okay but badly bruised." Fina raised her arms and put her hands to her head.

It was obvious from her flush face that the memories of these moments were difficult for her to recall.

Claire interrupted. "Julian still lives on top of the hill. That's who we are going to visit in a little while."

"Is he doing okay now?" Maurice asked.

"Yes, thankfully. A bit battered, but Fina told me last night he was doing better."

Claire got up from the table and went to the kitchen to get some more coffee. She also brought out some churros, those sugary fried pastries that Maurice liked so much.

Maurice sipped his coffee and ate a churro. "These are delicious. Perfect with coffee."

Fina glowed with pride. "My churros are the best in town. Have another!"

Claire waited for Maurice to finish and then said, "Here's where our story really begins."

She gave Maurice's arm a little tug. "Come with me outside."

Fina stayed inside and cleaned up the table while Claire and Maurice walked out to the street.

Claire walked Maurice up the street to the end of the block where the cobblestone ended. The street became nothing more than a dirt road that wound around and disappeared up a hill. It was flanked by wild shrubs and cactus.

Pointing toward the hill, Claire leaned close to Maurice. "That's where I want to take you this morning."

Maurice responded, "I know, you've mentioned it several times. I'm very curious what this is all about."

Claire sat down on an old tree stump. Maurice sat beside her.

"Well, as Fina said, eventually Julian took the money he had saved from work at the university and restored the old property on top of the hill. Shortly afterwards, a friend of his came to visit. His name is Euphrates, and he still lives there with Julian."

Claire noticed a curious look on Maurice's face when she mentioned his name.

"Yes, Euphrates. Unusual, isn't it? Well, so is he. He's deaf. Julian said he knew him from the time when he was a philosophy professor at the University of Granada. Euphrates was one of his brightest students."

Maurice asked, "What, you mean Julian taught in Granada, where I went?" He pressed his hand against his forehead. "What's his last name?" Maurice inquired excitedly.

"Bakkar, I think. Yes, Bakkar."

Maurice stared at the ground in deep thought. He took off his cap and tugged on his red curls. He was trying to think back if he had ever taken a course in philosophy while at the University of Granada. He didn't recognize his name, but after so many years and so many professors, he didn't trust his memory.

"Are we gonna meet Julian this morning? I really would like to meet him." He put his cap back on with renewed enthusiasm.

"Yes, let's head up there now. But just one thing … promise me that you'll remain open to new possibilities. The place that Julian has created is special, and he and Euphrates are particular about who they share it with. Hopefully, it should be apparent why."

At this point Maurice was overwhelmed by the events of the past twenty-four hours and the mystery of what he was about to experience.

Claire stood up and stretched. "Let's go, young man. It's a bit of a hike up there. Do you mind running back to tell Fina we're going up the hill?"

Maurice dashed to Fina's and came right back. He was anxious to see this place that Claire had been boasting about since they first met.

They walked slowly up the dirt road. Because of the heavy rains, there were places where the dirt had washed parts of the road away, leaving large ruts and potholes. They had to navigate carefully to avoid sinking ankle deep into the muddy holes.

Growing on either side of the road were pink and white oleander bushes in full bloom. Some wild Mediterranean fan palms and cacti completed the landscape. The poor soil and lack of moisture, except for the previous night's torrent, resulted in few, if any, trees being able to take root and survive.

They walked for a good ten minutes. The road slowly curved to the right, but Maurice still saw no structures of any kind in either direction, only what appeared to be an arid and empty landscape beyond the oleanders that lined the road.

"We're getting close." Claire was clearly winded and grabbed Maurice's arm to lean on. He put his arm around her to keep her steady, as the incline was quite severe. Claire responded by giving his arm a friendly squeeze.

As the road curved to the right, they came upon one of the old windmills, similar to the ones Maurice had seen on his drive across La Mancha the day before.

Maurice exclaimed, "Wow! I've always wanted to see one of these close up. They are much bigger than I would have thought."

Maurice stepped off the dirt road and ran up the hill another ten yards toward the windmill.

Claire yelled, "Hey, Maurice, come back and give me a hand. This old lady could use a rest."

Maurice ran back to Claire and held her arm as they both walked up to the steps of the old windmill. It was a cylindrical-shaped building made of adobelike material, and it was about twenty-five feet in diameter. With its tall cone-shaped roof, the entire structure stood at least forty feet tall. Its sail-less blades were supported by a mast that extended out of the roof at a forty-five-degree angle.

Claire said, "Let's sit here a minute. This seventy-year-old lady's engine doesn't get quite the mileage it used to."

"Seventy!" exclaimed Maurice. "You sure don't act your age."

With a childlike wink, she responded, "I try not to!"

Maurice brushed some fallen leaves and pebbles off the step with his hand. They made themselves comfortable.

Maurice looked up at the huge blades of the windmill that towered over them like the empty rigging of an old ship. The diameter of the windmill was at least thirty feet.

"Claire, I'm gonna see if the door is unlocked. I'd love to look inside." Maurice walked up to the large wooden door that stood at least ten feet high. He pushed it open far enough for him to squeeze through. Inside, he stood amongst a complex gear mechanism that filled the entire structure. For a moment he felt like a time traveler as he imagined the giant blades outside slowly spinning, activating the gears inside that would grind the grain.

The only light was that which came through the partially opened door, so he was reluctant to explore any further.

He stood just inside the doorway, trying to figure out how the mechanism must have functioned. He could have spent hours daydreaming about the simple but arduous life that the farmers endured centuries ago, but he knew Claire was waiting outside.

Maurice rejoined Claire on the steps.

Claire said to him, "You know, there's a curious tradition in town about this windmill. No one knows how it got started, but on your birthday you're supposed to walk up the hill and put some coins in the little water trough by the door of the windmill. In return you'll have good fortune until your next birthday. What they don't know is that every now and then Euphrates collects the coins and buys food supplies for the town's church to distribute to the needy. So I guess, in a sense, there is some truth to the legend."

Maurice was taking it all in. He stood up, reached into his pocket for a few coins, and dropped them in the trough.

He looked at Claire with a boyish grin and said, "That was for my last birthday." They laughed.

"Okay, ready to hit the trail again," she said, still a bit out of breath.

They resumed their walk. As the incline became steeper, they slowed down, until the road made a sudden turn to the right. Maurice still couldn't see any buildings but noticed that the road seemed to level off farther ahead.

Claire took Maurice's hand as they walked another ten yards to the top. Maurice stopped and made a 180-degree sweep of the horizon before him. He stood still, as he was mesmerized by the view before him. A sparkling blue ocean filled the horizon. Rows of brightly colored geraniums in shades of red, pink, purple, and white spilled over the rocks that marked the end of the road. To his far right he saw an old Spanish structure with a little turret partially hidden behind a tall white stucco wall. A stone walkway led to two huge carved wooden doors at least eight feet tall. On either side of the walkway, columns of cactus even taller than the doors stood guard like soldiers.

Maurice exclaimed, "It's breathtaking up here! One would never know this existed."

With a twinkle, Claire added, "That's the point."

She nudged him to continue walking.

They approached the huge wooden doors. The door on the left had an intricate carving of the sun, the other a rendering of a partial moon with a star above it. Below each carving was a large brass knob the size of Maurice's fist. Above the doors was a sign made of blue, yellow, and orange ceramic tiles. It spelled "ASILOMAR."

"Asilomar," Maurice said. He repeated, "Asilomar," trying to decipher its meaning.

"Translated from Spanish, it literally means 'asylum' or 'refuge by the sea,'" Claire said as she pointed out toward the ocean.

"Yes, it's a … uh … oh, yeah, it's what's called a portmanteau, two words blended together to make a new one." Maurice turned to Claire with a smile on his face. He enjoyed showing off his literary prowess.

"Well, port-whatever, it lives up to its name." Claire walked over to the right side of the door and opened up a little wooden latch the size of a mailbox. She had to stand on her toes and reach up, as the latch was just above eye level. She tugged on the little handle, revealing a simple doorbell.

She chuckled as she pressed it. "I guess a little modern technology doesn't hurt. Julian never locks this gate, but I like to ring the bell so I don't surprise anyone."

Maurice removed his hat and performed the usual ritual of twirling his hair with his fingers.

They waited for a minute or so. Claire rang the bell a second time.

Seconds later, they heard what sounded like someone moving a latch, and the doors vibrated for a second.

The right door creaked as it slowly swung open.

"Julian!" Claire lunged to embrace the slender gentleman standing before her. He had a large bandage across his forehead that partially covered his right eye, which was swollen and discolored.

Julian held Claire in a tentative embrace, as he was clearly still in some pain from his episode of a few days earlier.

As was the style of many men in Spain, Julian sported short dark hair with a few days' growth of a beard. He was of dark complexion, just as Fina had described. On closer inspection, his face was badly scratched and his right hand was swollen and wrapped in a bandage.

"How's my Claire doing? It's great to see you. Fina told me you arrived late due to the storm."

"I'm great, Jules. It's wonderful to be back."

Maurice noticed Claire's endearing nickname for Julian.

"So, is this the young lad who came to your rescue?" Julian wrapped his left arm around Claire's shoulder. He started to extend his other arm to greet Maurice but recoiled as he realized his hand was still wrapped in bandages.

Claire introduced Maurice, "Yes, this is Maurice. Maurice, Julian."

"Very nice to meet you, Julian. Claire has already told me quite a bit about you." Maurice stood awkwardly after Julian's aborted handshake.

Julian quickly replied, "Oh, I bet she did. If you haven't discovered already, Claire is a wealth of information, and she doesn't hesitate to share it." Maurice noticed Julian grimace in pain as he grinned.

"Sorry, my face isn't quite back together yet. Come on in, let's get comfortable, and then I'll show Maurice around."

Maurice couldn't help but notice how Julian had made continuous eye contact with him. In spite of a badly bruised face, his eyes reflected a calmness that made him feel welcome. After their introduction, Maurice was confident that he had never attended one of Julian's classes.

Claire and Julian walked with their arms locked. Julian was wearing a worn pair of jeans and blue tennis shoes. Underneath his unbuttoned short-sleeve shirt was a body-hugging white tank top revealing Julian's good physical shape, increasing the probability that his attackers may have at least felt some of their own medicine.

Maurice followed but couldn't take his eyes off the gardens that were hidden behind the wall. The flowering bushes and trees, and exotic palms and cactus were in stark contrast to the wildness of the surrounding landscape. It was a world of colors, textures, and fragrances that he had never experienced.

He stopped to take a deep breath, trying to capture and identify the various scents in the air. He could hear water moving. A soft gurgling sound came from between a clump of palms. He stepped a few feet off the path and peeked over some flowers. He uttered in a low tone, "Wow," as he discovered a stone basin at the foot of a moss-covered wall. Above the basin was a figure of a dragon embedded in the wall. Water slowly flowed from the dragon's mouth. Maurice was mesmerized.

Realizing he had fallen behind, Maurice dashed through the winding path to catch up to Clair and Julian, who had just reached the front door to the house. Carved in a large wooden beam above the door was the word, "ASILOMAR."

The door creaked as Julian opened it. It too was adorned, but its geometric carvings were less dramatic than those on the front gate. As they entered, their eyes had to adjust from the bright sunlight. Expecting to walk into a living area, Maurice was surprised to find himself in an enclosed reception foyer. An old wooden desk with books and papers neatly stacked on one corner was directly in front of them. Behind the desk were various postings on the wall, but Maurice still wasn't able to read them, as his eyes still hadn't adjusted. His attention was caught by a long and narrow hallway that veered to the right. There was nothing special about it other than the bright sunlight that shone like a headlight at the far end, where it exited to the outside.

Claire motioned to Maurice to follow Julian. They walked through the short hallway whose walls were bare except for several picture frames. Again, Maurice didn't pay too much attention to them. In the middle of the hallway on either side were narrow doorways, each with a wood door. At the end of the hall was an archway leading again to a sun-drenched patio.

Julian stopped at the end of the hall and told Maurice, "Make yourself comfortable on the patio, Maurice. I'll get some refreshments for us. Would you like some wine or beer? We have juice too."

"A beer sounds great, thanks." He realized it was still late morning, but after the trek up the hill it sounded too good to resist.

"Great, that sounds good. I'll have one too." Maurice felt more comfortable that he didn't have to drink alone. "Claire, my dear, the usual?" Julian was a gracious host.

"Yes, thanks, Jules," replied Claire as she took a seat on one of the wide rattan chairs with bright-orange cushions.

Before sitting down, Maurice walked around the large patio that was bordered on two sides by the house—one side from which they entered through the arched hallway, and another where French doors led to the kitchen.

The rest of the patio was bordered by a low stucco wall about four feet high. In one direction Maurice could see a group of small white stucco buildings with red tile roofs. They were huddled in a circle with a large lawn in the middle. A bit farther off in the distance it appeared there was an iron fence surrounding another garden area. Beyond the lush gardens one could see the encroaching wilderness that surrounded Asilomar. A rocky and barren mountainside appeared to wrap around all sides of the peaceful oasis except for that which faced toward the ocean.

Past the far end of the patio there appeared to be nothing but blue sky. Maurice walked to the edge and said, "Oh my gosh, this is incredible." Beneath him the ocean stretched unobstructed to the horizon. He stood there, frozen for a moment, as he had when he had first seen the picturesque house at the end of the road.

Claire walked up behind him. "This is Asilomar, Maurice. Refuge by the sea."

Maurice added, "Yes, it definitely is!"

Maurice and Claire took a seat by the table a few feet away. Julian came through the French doors carrying a tray of refreshments.

"Your home is absolutely exquisite, Julian. There is such peace here. It's hard to describe the feeling it creates." He wasn't even aware that he was no longer wearing his hat, and at least for the moment, he wasn't self-conscious that his red curls were disheveled from the breeze.

"Thank you, Maurice. *Salud.* Welcome again to Asilomar."

They raised and clanked their glasses together, the sound briefly interrupting the quiet on the patio. Claire drank her "usual," which appeared to be juice of some sort.

"What are you drinking, Claire?" Maurice asked.

"Oh, it's a special concoction that Jules makes for me—a combination of pomegranate, orange, and kaki juice. Kaki is a fruit that grows locally here—quite juicy and sweet. We know it in the United States as persimmon. Keeps this old lady humming." They laughed.

At that moment Sucre ran out to the patio, panting from her long run up the hill. She walked up to Claire and licked her hand. She then made the rounds to Julian and finally to Maurice. She settled down and lay down between Julian and Maurice, with her head resting on Maurice's foot.

"She likes you, I can tell." Julian leaned back in his chair and looked at Maurice, as if making a quick study of him. "Claire told me a little bit about you," Julian commented as he lifted his beer to his lips. He too had strong hands, but the weathered skin and veins defied his otherwise youthful appearance. "You went to University of Granada I understand?"

"Well, yes, for my junior year abroad. It was a great experience. I haven't been back in nearly ten years. That's where I'm headed now." Maurice's eyes widened, as he was still surprised at how much everyone knew about him.

"Yes, so you're a *botellonista*, eh?" Groups of young people in Spain, particularly at the universities, would gather at midnight in parks or plazas with bottles of alcohol. They would drink and party until sunrise. It was more economical than paying high prices at bars or clubs. The term *botellón* or *botellonista* referred to the "bottles" they brought with them to drink.

Maurice shook his head. "I participated once, but I just couldn't handle that much alcohol."

Julian continued, "Well, Claire may have told you that I was a professor there in philosophy for a number of years, but it sounds like it was probably after you attended."

"Yes, but what a coincidence," Maurice replied.

Julian commented, "Perhaps not a coincidence."

Maurice heard Julian's comment but let it pass. He was impressed and curious about Asilomar, but he instinctively wanted to resume his planned schedule.

Maurice added, "I'm planning to spend a couple of weeks in Granada—sort of a ten-year reunion. I guess I should start back in a couple of hours to get there before dark."

Julian glanced at Claire with a little frown. "I thought you said Maurice was going to be our guest for a while."

Maurice looked at Claire with a friendly glare.

"Oh, I believe he is. Aren't you, Maurice?" Claire looked back at Maurice with an equally intense stare.

Maurice again was surprised at how his itinerary continued to slip out of his control. But what surprised him more was that he wasn't resisting like he thought he would. Having seen how beautiful Asilomar was, it didn't take much convincing. Maurice did add, "Well, I need to contact my hotel then and let them know that I'll be delayed longer than I had expected."

Claire didn't hesitate to add, "That's already been taken care of, dear."

Her little face wrinkled up with a little smirk. As devious as she was, Maurice couldn't help but smile and say, "You're not the innocent lady I thought you were when I picked you up on that highway, Ms. Claire."

Julian added, "I'll drink to that!" They raised their glasses and joined in a good laugh.

Claire excused herself. As she got up, Julian said, "Claire, your regular *casita* is all ready for you. Rest up and we'll see you later for dinner. I'll have Euphrates go down to Fina's to pick up your luggage.

Claire left, leaving Maurice to wonder about Euphrates. That was the first mention of him, and he didn't appear to be around.

Maurice noticed that Julian pulled his chair closer, perhaps in anticipation of a more focused conversation.

Surprisingly, Maurice took the initiative to start. "Julian, may I ask how you and Claire met?"

"Sure. I don't know if you were aware, but Claire's husband was a well-known jazz musician. Years ago he and his trio were part of a music festival at the university. I was a member of the sponsoring committee that helped to organize it." Julian took a slow sip of his beer and wiped a little foam from of his beard-stubbled face.

Julian continued to explain that shortly after his performance he suffered a major stroke from which he never really recovered. He helped to arrange a prolonged hospital stay in Granada and grew close to Claire during that time, as she was devastated and had little emotional support available to her in a city thousands of miles from home. She spent long days at her husband's side for almost three weeks. The diagnosis wasn't positive, but they decided to transfer him to a hospital in the United States. He passed a month later. Julian stayed in touch with Claire and invited her to visit, thinking it would be cathartic for her to recover from her loss where she last remembered her husband as a healthy man. He explained how skeptical she was at first but a year later decided to come.

Maurice commented, "That must have been very difficult for her and, of course, very generous of you."

"It's not a matter of generosity. I see us all as connected. I believe in karma. I believe the less pain that an individual feels, then the less pain we all feel. I felt that Claire had a destiny of her own that needed to be fulfilled. She had always lived in the shadow of her husband, and I wanted to help her to visualize and realize some of her own dreams and aspirations."

There was a long pause in the conversation as both men enjoyed the refreshing coolness of their beers, each staring off in different directions. Julian was nurturing, comforting, and professorial at the same time. He spoke very good English except for a pronounced accent from having grown up speaking mostly French and Moroccan Arabic.

"We'll talk more about Claire a little later. I'll let her explain her Asilomar story firsthand. Can I get you another beer, Maurice?" He chuckled as he added, "Since you won't have to worry about driving anywhere for a while."

"Sure, thanks, Julian. Oh, where's your restroom?"

"It's down the hallway where you came in. The door on the right."

Maurice got up and entered the hallway. It was dark, and it took a few minutes for his eyes to adjust from the bright light on the patio. He found the bathroom, which was tiled with Moorish designs around the sink and shower. The walls were done in a finish reminiscent of *tadelakt*, or plaster made from lime quarried in Marrakech, Morocco. He recognized the style from architectural magazines he had read. The plaster was rubbed and sealed into a weathered opaque and waterproof finish. It was common in the riads, or palaces, of Morocco. The mirror above the basin was framed in blue, green, and purple tile. Above it hung a little sign. It read, "Your Dreams May Be Closer Than They Appear." He thought it was cute. As he left the bathroom, he couldn't help but notice the picture frame on the wall in the hallway.

Inside the ornate frame, about the size of a diploma, was a simple statement printed in bold calligraphy. It read, "If you share a secret, do you think it will alter your destiny?" And beneath the statement, it was signed, "Omar Ibn Al-Khattab 634 CE."

He noticed another frame farther down the hallway but thought he should head back out to visit with his host. *I'll have time later to explore,* he thought to himself.

He rejoined Julian, who at this point had left the patio table and was sitting on the ledge overlooking the ocean.

Julian looked up as Maurice sat next to him. They both paused for a second. Maurice felt self-conscious that he had been staring at the cuts and bruises on Julian's face and neck. He became aware that Julian may have been looking at his red hair.

Maurice broke the awkward silence. "Man, they really did a number on you, Julian."

"Yeah, they got the better of me. Unfortunately, I know they'll be back to try again. But that's negative stuff. We can address that some other time." It was clear that Julian didn't feel like talking about the beating incident.

Changing the subject, Julian asked, "Maurice, how much has Claire told you about Asilomar?"

"Well, she didn't go into a lot of detail. We talked about the very name, Asilomar, and what it meant. She said this had been her pilgrimage for years, to relax and unwind."

Julian explained that Asilomar was much more than a place to relax. It was a refuge, yes, but not to hide. It was more a place of self-discovery, a place where personal self-restraints, doubts, and fears can be exposed, addressed, and forgotten. Julian used the analogy of a hot air balloon that throws out the ballast and rises above the noise and distortion below.

"Yes, I can see how this place offers a safe environment for self-reflection. Claire told me during our drive that she comes here regularly for what she called 'open soul surgery.'"

Julian chuckled. "Ah, Claire can be dramatic. But you know it is about opening your soul to the sunlight, letting it be refreshed and energized."

Julian lifted his arm and pointed out to the sea. "This view and the peaceful setting is what kept me here. The sea appears endless, as I hope life's possibilities are." He reached down to pick up the beer he had set beneath him on the patio floor.

After a long sip, he added, "Now don't get me wrong, I'm a realist too. We're all works in progress, and some hurdles are very difficult, if not impossible, to overcome. But trying is 99 percent."

As Julian spoke, Maurice found himself drawn in by his philosophy.

"You know, Julian, I came to Spain for a two-week trip. It was somewhat disguised as a class reunion in Granada, but in reality I knew I needed to go somewhere far away, alone, and on my own initiative. I guess I'm still not entirely sure why I …"

Maurice reached for his beer. He paused, fearing he would say something stupid.

"Entirely sure why …?" Julian inquired.

Drops of moisture trickled down Maurice's cheek. It was warm in the sun despite the slight ocean breeze, but it was his nerves that were making him sweat. It was unlike him to open up to a person he met barely an hour before. He wiped the beads of moisture with his sleeve.

Maurice stared out at the open sea for a moment. Feeling a bit put on the spot, his nervous tic was about to return, but he stopped himself before his hand reached the top of his head.

He continued, "I guess I feel lost in some ways. I have this urge inside that there is something more for me than routine and predictability," Maurice confessed.

Julian chuckled. "You know, you're sounding a lot like Claire did years ago. Yes, sometimes we fall captive to fear and doubt. It paralyzes ... it truly does." Finishing off his beer, Julian added, "Claire was one of our first guests here."

Maurice decided it was his turn to ask some questions.

"What do you do here, Julian? Do you write? Research? It's such a large place to take care of too."

Julian obliged with an answer. "Well, as I said, Asilomar is more than a refuge. We have guests from time to time who seek us out or who have been referred by someone like Claire. They generally are folks who need healing, redirection, personal growth, guidance to overcome a fear or to pursue a dream."

Maurice's eyes widened.

Julian looked directly at Maurice and said, "But let me be clear. Contrary to what some townspeople and others may think, we *do not* perform miracles. After all, miracles are the rare end product of sitting and passively waiting for something to happen. Achieving a dream or something special takes visualization, motivation, a plan of pursuit, and a willingness to fail."

Maurice nodded. He was impressed with how Julian was able to articulate things so simply and clearly.

Julian continued, "At Asilomar we surround our guests in an uninhibited atmosphere of encouragement where there is no one around to cast doubt on their hopes and dreams. There's no promotion or advertising. When people visit, it's usually because they are drawn here for the right reasons. I like to say we are well-known to those who know us well."

"I understand," replied Maurice.

"There are five cabins—or casitas, as we call them—next door for guests. We provide breakfast and sometimes dinner. It all depends on who is here and what their needs are."

Maurice was about to say something but hesitated. Julian motioned for him to continue.

Maurice said with reserve, "I noticed you continue to say 'we.' Claire mentioned there's another gentleman who lives here ... uh ..."

Julian stood up and turned. "Ah, the timing couldn't be better."

Walking across the patio toward them was a tall, slender, and olive-skinned man wearing long baggy pants and a Moroccan tunic-style shirt.

"Maurice, this is Euphrates. He's deaf, so we sign. He is my business partner and closest friend."

Maurice reached to shake Euphrates's hand. Even though quite different from other sign languages, Maurice wished he had continued to study American Sign Language (ASL) when he dated a deaf man years ago. He thought it still might help him communicate some basic expressions.

Awkwardly, Maurice said, "Hello, Euphrates, it's a pleasure to meet you." He hoped that he was able to read his lips.

Euphrates extended his long arms and grasped Maurice's hand tightly and gave it a firm shake. His face remained nearly expressionless, cracking only a slight smile of politeness. His large almond-shaped eyes were dark, and his eyebrows were thick and black like his short but curly hair.

Maurice returned an awkward smile in response to Euphrates's mysterious and intimidating presence.

Euphrates turned and started signing to Julian. His arms and hands moved deliberately and smoothly, as if conducting a silent symphony. His coordinated facial expressions added a level of complexity that caused Maurice to unconsciously stare.

"No thanks, Pacha, we've finished. We need to show Maurice to his cabin." Julian was verbal for Maurice's benefit but continued to sign, as well. Julian turned to Maurice and said, "Euphrates primarily signs in LSE, which is Spain's version of sign language. Euphrates disappeared into the kitchen.

Julian turned to Maurice and said, "I call him Pacha, which is a nickname he said he had when he was a child. But he prefers everyone else call him Euphrates. While I've learned sign language over the years, we still need to exchange notes from time to time." Julian continued, "His father was from northern Spain, and his mother was from Morocco. He can read and write in Spanish and English and knows a little Moroccan Arabic, as well. He is very proud of his Spanish and Moroccan heritage." Julian tapped Maurice on the shoulder and said, "Come with me, Maurice. I'll show you to your casita."

They walked across the patio and out a small gate. They followed along another flower-lined path that led them to the cluster of five little Spanish-styled buildings, each with tiled roofs, tall wood shutters covering the windows, and small arched entryways. The casitas were identified by a tile number over the front door: 1, 2, 3, 4, and 5.

They stopped in front of Casita 3.

"Here's your new home for a while, Maurice. Again, we're glad to have you at Asilomar. I hope you take advantage of everything while you're here. We thought we'd have dinner on the patio around eight, just as the sun is setting. Euphrates is a great cook!" Julian gave Maurice a generous hug and started to turn away.

Maurice said, "Julian, you are so kind, but I really don't want to impose since it was Claire that you were expecting."

Julian walked up close to Maurice and put his hands on Maurice's shoulders. "Maurice, you are exactly where you are supposed to be."

Julian walked back to the main house. Maurice felt a tingle resonate throughout his body. He felt something very special was about to happen to him.

He found his suitcase waiting inside his little house. He opened the shutters covering his windows. The smells of the garden rushed in. He was exhausted and fell asleep across the bed.

Maurice woke up startled. For a second he had forgotten where he was as he lay across the bed, looking around at his unfamiliar surroundings.

His room was comfortable but sparsely furnished. Old wood beams stretched across the ceiling above him. The wide wood plank flooring revealed the heavy traffic that it had withstood over the years. Its long history seeped from the floorboards as Maurice imagined all the interesting people who must have walked on them. The white plaster walls were bare except for a small framed watercolor of a sunrise over the ocean. Upon closer inspection, it appeared to be a likeness of Asilomar's patio. In the lower right-hand corner was the artist's signature: "Clifford Easton." He thought nothing of it at the time, as he had suddenly realized that he needed to go to dinner.

"Uh-oh," he said to himself. "What time is it? I hope I didn't miss dinner."

He quickly pulled out his cell phone and checked the local time.

"Good, it's only five." Relieved that his nap had been shorter than he feared, he got up, took just what he needed out of his suitcase, jumped in the shower, and got dressed. After seeing how casual Julian and Euphrates were dressed, he decided to put on another pair of jeans and pullover shirt with a hood in case it got chilly. "No cap tonight," he decided.

After he finished getting dressed, he noticed his notepad had fallen out of his jacket pocket onto the floor. Instead of quickly scrambling to pick it up, he stared at it for a minute.

Gosh, he thought, *I haven't written down any notes since yesterday.*

He was surprised that he had fallen out of his routine of writing notes—and even more that he hadn't realized it until then. He bent over, picked up the notepad, and put it on top of his suitcase. "I'll catch up with some of this later tonight," he promised himself.

With a couple of hours left before dinner, Maurice figured he had some time to explore Asilomar. He recalled the little garden he had seen tucked away in the distance, and he wanted to revisit the entrance where they first came into the house.

As soon as he stepped out the door, he knew he had arrived at a special place. The smells that captured his attention earlier had become more intense with the approach of evening. The moisture from the sea air seemed to hold captive the fragrance of jasmine and citrus. He took a deep breath. The sun was getting lower in the sky, and the warmth of the day had surrendered to the cool freshness of the early evening. He was glad he put on his hooded shirt.

He hesitated by the doorway for a few moments, not sure which way to go. The little casitas were set in a circle with a curved pathway that connected all the buildings. The grassy area in the middle didn't seem as well manicured as the rest of the garden but was very green. All the casitas looked alike except for one distinguishing characteristic. Each one had a different kind of tree in front of it. In front of his there was a small but ornamental tree with flowers of different shades—deep blue, light blue, and pale white. They had no fragrance, but the combination of different shades of flower on the same bush was curious.

He turned to his left and approached neighboring Casita 4. It had a lemon tree by the front door. Since the shutters were closed, it wasn't apparent if it was occupied or not. Proceeding to Casita 5, he noticed the shutters were open. He caught a glimpse of Claire through the narrow window. He didn't feel like conversation just then, so he continued his walk, noticing that the short tree by her casita had orange fruits that were shaped like bell peppers. They looked vaguely familiar, but he wasn't sure what they were.

As he circled the wide open lawn, he came to Casitas 1 and 2. Again, their shutters were closed. He recognized a guava tree in front of 1. There was an orange tree in front of 2.

Having completed the little circle, Maurice wondered if he and Claire were the only guests. He figured it would become apparent at dinnertime.

He followed the main path back toward the house. He couldn't quite remember where the little garden was that he glimpsed from a distance from the patio. As he got closer to the house, he noticed there was another little path that veered off to the right. He hoped that it would lead him there.

As he was about to turn down the path, he heard Claire yell out to him, "Maurice, wait up."

Maurice turned around, trying not to show his disappointment that she interrupted his self-tour of Asilomar.

Walking her usual brisk and determined gait, she caught up and gave him a big hug.

"What do you think so far, dear? She's quite beautiful and inspiring, isn't she?" Claire reached out and wrapped her arm around Maurice's.

"Yes, I never would have imagined such a place except in my dreams." Maurice noted how Claire described Asilomar, using the proper pronoun "she."

"Ah, like a dream … more than you may think." She had that twinkle in her eye that usually meant she was up to something.

"Did you have a nice talk with Julian? Did you meet Euphrates?" she inquired, still holding onto his arm.

"Yes, Julian is amazing. He has created something very special here. I'm still not quite sure how to describe it but—"

Claire made her typical interruption. "Don't worry. It will all become apparent in time. Asilomar is not just a place, it's an experience. A state of mind."

Maurice added, "And I met Euphrates too. He walked up just as we were finishing our beers. He seemed nice but was very quiet. I almost felt like I was intruding."

"Oh, no, don't think that at all. Euphrates—he's deaf, you know … oh, of course you know—but I do think he can hear more than he lets on. He is very quiet and reserved until he gets to know you. He's very loyal and protective of Julian and would do almost anything for him."

"He is very handsome, isn't he?" Maurice noticed Claire wink. "He does look older than he is—only twenty-nine. How old are you, Maurice?"

Maurice answered, "Thirty-three."

"Oh, my, I would have guessed you were younger. Good genes." Claire chuckled.

Maurice wasn't really bothered by Claire's conversation, but he was surprised that Euphrates was only twenty-nine. He tried not to look interested, but he did want to know more about Euphrates.

"Uh, are they partners? I mean romantic partners?" Maurice ran his fingers through his curls once again, not sure if it was appropriate to ask such a personal question.

"No, they're just very close friends. Euphrates admires Julian for his kindness, generosity, and, of course, his intellect. He also feels indebted to him for giving him the opportunity to be part of Asilomar." Claire added with a mischievous smile, "Julian is straight as an arrow. Now Euphrates, I think you may have something in common there."

Although Maurice was getting accustomed to Claire's boldness, her observations about his sexuality surprised him.

Claire explained that several years after Euphrates's graduation from the university, they ran into one another at a café in nearby Almería. Euphrates had left his job as an editor of the university newspaper and was unsure of what he wanted to do. Julian invited him to help him finish renovating his property and perhaps create some guesthouses and a little café to bring in some income.

"Where were you headed?" asked Claire.

"Just touring the grounds. Actually, this morning I thought I had seen a little garden hidden away in the corner of the yard." Maurice pointed toward the lush area on the other side of the lawn.

"Yes, let's go. It's the most peaceful spot on the whole property. It was Euphrates's creation. I'll show you."

As they started down the path, Maurice felt something bump on his leg. It was Sucre, eager to join their walk.

"That pooch really has something for you. Dogs have a sense about people, and they are rarely mistaken." Claire reached down and rubbed Sucre's head.

It wasn't very far before they encountered a five-foot iron fence that was partially covered with flowering vines. The fence enclosed an area about twenty-five feet square. Most of it was concealed by lush vegetation. The path turned slightly to reveal a taller iron gate with two black iron lanterns attached on either side.

Maurice looked at Claire, as if waiting for permission to enter. Claire waved him on to open the gate.

The gate creaked like in the old scary movies, but what lay beyond was anything but dark and foreboding. Within moments of entering, one could hear water running. From one direction it was a trickling sound, like water dripping into a pool. From another direction the sound was a bit more intense, as if there was a small creek flowing over rocks.

Directly in front of them was a large fountain, much like one would expect in the middle of a small Spanish plaza. It had three different levels, with water gently making its way from an obscure opening at the top, cascading through two different bowls, and ending in a pool that surrounded the fountain.

It was the unique shape of the pool that Maurice found striking.

If viewed from above it would have looked like a circle but with four points protruding equidistantly around the circle. It was, in fact, a compass. Each point was marked by a blue ceramic tile representing the direction—in this case N, S, E, and O (*oeste*, Spanish for "west"). Maurice was enchanted with the garden. He loved spending hours working in his own desert garden back in Las Vegas, but the lushness of this private paradise left him speechless.

"Let's sit down and enjoy the feeling here." It was obvious from Claire's enthusiasm that she enjoyed showing off Asilomar.

Across from each directional point there was a crude wooden bench, more than likely carved out of old tree trunks. They were cracked, and their legs were covered in moss.

Maurice said, "This is like a secret garden, isn't it? Like out of a fairy tale?"

"Kinda," Claire answered. "Except it has a very important meaning to both Euphrates and Julian."

Claire continued to explain that a year or so after he moved to Asilomar, Julian recognized the love Euphrates had for nature and Asilomar's surroundings. He had planted much of the landscape prior to his arrival but said that Euphrates had noticed a bare section of land about thirty yards from the patio. He asked Julian if he could do something special there as a thank-you for all that he had done for him. Julian was both touched and happy that Euphrates felt at home and wanted to contribute something lasting to Asilomar.

"He did this all by himself?" Maurice asked in amazement. He was still playing with a pink hibiscus blossom that he had picked off a bush as they entered the garden.

"I know the design and ideas were his, but some of the young men in town helped with the actual construction. In fact, one of the earlier visitors to Asilomar made the wooden benches." Claire suggested, "Maurice, walk around the fountain and let me know if you see anything unusual." She motioned with her hands for him to walk around and investigate.

He slowly walked around the fountain, as Claire had not so subtly instructed. He made one revolution around the entire fountain. One obvious thing he noted was that there were no coins in the basin, as one would expect in most fountains. Other than that there was nothing else that stood out as unusual.

Claire said, "Walk around again, and this time notice the edges of the basin."

"Okay, but I feel like I'm on a treasure hunt," he replied.

"We all are," responded Claire without hesitation.

Maurice continued walking. Suddenly he stopped. He bent over and looked more closely on the ground next to the edge of the basin.

"I don't know how I missed that the first time," he confessed.

Near his foot, halfway between the "S" and "E" markers, was a smaller tile that had the letters "JTB." He looked up at Claire, as if expecting a quick explanation. Claire motioned for him to keep walking.

He walked a bit more, passing the "E" marker and then the "N" marker. After a few more steps he noticed another little tile on the ground. It had the letters "EB." He completed the circle without seeing any additional tile markers.

He looked up at Claire. "I guess I'm ready for my next lesson," he joked. "What is the significance of the compass design, and especially the little tiles with initials?"

Before Claire could answer, they heard the gate opening. It was Euphrates. He approached Claire and Maurice. He gave Claire a hug and kissed both cheeks. As Euphrates smiled, his modestly thick lips revealed glistening white teeth. His eyes squinted as his cheeks widened to accommodate his wide grin.

Maurice thought he was cute … and sexy.

Maurice stood up to greet Euphrates, and they both extended their arms and clasped hands. It was a pleasant greeting but certainly not the warm reception that Claire had received.

As they shook hands, Maurice could not help but notice the aroma of incense. It must have been on his shirt, he thought. The scent was as exotic as his unique mix of Spanish and Moroccan features.

Maurice looked at Claire, as if to ask for help in how to communicate with him.

She offered, "He can read lips a little, but he needs to spend more time with a person to sense their speech patterns. I've always been amazed that he can read lips in several languages—that is, once he knows where you're from."

Euphrates was wearing the same type of Moroccan shirt that he wore earlier, only this one was more colorful and the neckline was a bit lower, revealing curls of dark black hair on his chest.

As Euphrates stood in front of Maurice, he motioned with his open arms toward the house.

At that moment they heard the sound of a deep but pleasant-sounding chime coming from the house.

Euphrates signaled both of them to return to the house.

Claire said, "That's the signal for dinner." She followed Euphrates.

Maurice lagged behind, staring for a moment at the fountain that was covered with dappled sunlight shining low beneath the trees.

He reflected on what a peaceful but unusual place this was. He mumbled to himself, "Why did Julian think I was meant to be here?"

He didn't have time to ponder his question, as Claire turned around and yelled with a friendly laugh, "C'mon, Maurice. Don't get lost back there."

Secrets Shared

*E*uphrates showed Maurice and Claire to their seats, one on each side of the rectangular table. It was long enough to seat two people on each side, but tonight they had room to spread out, as there were no other guests. The ends of the table were obviously reserved for Julian and Euphrates.

The air was heavy with the smell of salt from the ocean below and the sweet scent of night-blooming jasmine. The glow in the sky was orange-pink from the sun that was just minutes above the horizon. Two small torches were lit on either side of the patio. Asilomar was like no other place that Maurice had ever experienced. It was as unconventional as it was enchanting. That evening captured the essence of what one would expect in a magical daydream.

The wooden plank table was set very simply with colorful place mats and plain but attractive silverware. A big glass goblet sat in front of every place setting. There was a small brightly painted ceramic vase in the middle filled with freshly cut flowers, including some of the ones from the tree in front of Maurice's casita.

Julian had prepared a typical Spanish tapa as a preamble to dinner: anchovies on top of slices of ham and cheese, drizzled in olive oil. Maurice cringed internally upon seeing the anchovies, as this was all so new to his unchallenged taste buds. After taking a small bite, out of politeness, he found himself enjoying the way the salty ham and anchovy contrasted with the fruity silkiness of the olive oil.

Euphrates went back to the kitchen and quickly returned with bread and a bottle of wine.

Julian filled each of the large goblets about halfway with wine and quietly sat down. He tapped lightly on the table to get Euphrates's attention and raised his glass to lead his guests in a toast.

"We give a warm welcome to our special guests, Claire and Maurice. May your journeys be long, and may your dreams be forever. *Salud.*"

At the same time Julian was speaking, Euphrates was signing the same toast.

The quiet of the evening was broken by the gentle *ting ting* of goblets saluting Julian's welcome toast.

Maurice was momentarily distracted, staring out toward the ocean.

"Are you okay, Maurice?" inquired his host.

"Oh, I'm sorry. Just caught up in the moment, I guess." Maurice was hesitant to admit that Julian's toast had an especially poignant meaning for him, but he couldn't disguise the reflective look on his face.

"Maurice, one thing you'll learn here is that it's safe to discuss just about anything, particularly if it concerns any aspect of your journey, the reason you find yourself here tonight."

Still awed by the perceptive powers of Julian, Maurice made a small confession.

"Julian, your toast resonated with me in an almost surreal way. Coincidence, I guess." Maurice hesitated.

"Well, perhaps not," added Julian, whose expression was full of anticipation.

He reached into his shirt and pulled out a metal tag that was attached to a silver chain around his neck.

All three were looking at Maurice. He heard Claire mumble, "Yes, yes?"

Maurice said, "I found this at a shop a few years ago. When I was packing, I saw it in my jewelry box and decided to wear it."

He read from the little tag: "When you set out on the voyage to Ithaca, pray that your journey may be long, full of adventure, full of knowledge."

Julian clasped his hands in front of his face. "Yes, the Greek poem by Cavafy."

Julian signed the inscription on the tag to Euphrates, who clapped his hands to show his approval. He understood the significance of the tag that Maurice was wearing.

"Yes," responded Maurice. "It's so similar to your toast. I'm still reeling from the coincidence."

"Again, perhaps it's not all coincidence, Maurice. Remember, I said earlier you are where you're supposed to be." Julian added, "Let's eat and enjoy a relaxing dinner. I think we have some interesting things to talk about this evening." His eyes were focused on Maurice.

Euphrates left the table. Moments later he came out of the kitchen with a huge pan of paella. Julian moved the vase of flowers so he could put the large round pan in the middle of the table. It was steaming, and the aroma of saffron and seafood quickly replaced that of the jasmine.

Everyone helped themselves to the paella, which was topped with whole shrimp and baby squid. Claire remarked that Euphrates's culinary skills seemed to get better every year.

"But wait until you taste dessert," Julian responded. He looked toward Euphrates and signed.

Euphrates nodded and put his fingers to his lips and smiled.

Julian commented, "That's the dessert master over there."

Conversation over dinner was light and general. Claire updated Julian that she was going to sign over her property in Hawaii to her nephew, since her husband and only child had passed away. She was trying to settle things and simplify, adding that she didn't know how much longer she would be coming to Asilomar.

Julian interrupted, "Claire, you keep coming here as long as you have breath in your lungs. You're never too old to learn something new at Asilomar."

"Oh, Jules, I'll be back. But about learning something new, I'm at that stage where I've forgotten more than I'll ever learn," she joked.

Maurice and Julian laughed.

"Oh, you know I'm kidding," she confessed.

After finishing off second helpings of paella and refills of the wine goblets, everyone was ready to pause and let the food settle.

Julian invited Claire and Maurice to pick a lounge chair and get comfortable. "Euphrates and I will make some coffee and bring out the dessert."

The two hosts soon returned with their bounty of sweets and coffee. The smell of espresso that wafted across the patio competed with all the other aromas of that evening. Maurice even detected the scent of incense, perhaps coming from the house or maybe infused in Euphrates's clothing. Either way, it was a delightful mix that played with his senses.

The four of them sat quietly for a few moments. They enjoyed watching the orange sky take on a purple hew and then quietly fade to darkness.

Julian interrupted the silence. "You know, a day doesn't go by where I don't look around and appreciate all of this, including friends and visitors like you and Claire." Maurice noticed how he phrased the sentence to be directed at him. He continued, "Maurice, you're obviously on some sort of journey of repair … self-realization … fulfillment. Do you know why you're here?"

Maurice was caught off guard by Julian's direct question but responded as best he could. "To be honest, no. Well, let me clarify. I know that I need to eject some of the baggage that may be holding me back from things that I dream about. But no, I don't know why I ended up at Asilomar."

Julian signed for Euphrates while Maurice was talking.

Julian commented, "We are all on our individual journeys. That's why I like those flowers in the vase over there. All from the same bush but different colors."

"I noticed those by my casita," remarked Maurice.

Julian replied, "Yes, in English I believe they are called 'yesterday, today, and tomorrow.' I like that. The first day they're dark blue. The next day they lighten up to a softer blue. The third day they are almost white. Sort of like us, changing and getting brighter as we move forward." He continued, "There is no right or wrong answer, Maurice, but your response is the right one for someone who has found Asilomar. I hope over the course of time that you're here you'll experience a process of discovery."

Maurice nodded but said to Julian, "You know I had only planned a short vacation. We haven't talked about the logistics of staying here—how much it costs, is there room for me, how long—"

Julian interrupted, "Maurice, logistics are logistics, the least important and easiest to resolve. You will pay what you can afford. Yes, we have room. And we'll find a way for you to stay as long as you want. There's always a solution to these things."

Maurice nodded. "Thanks, Julian. This is all new to me. I really want to be part of this experience. I just don't know where to start."

"You already have," Julian said.

Maurice again had the urge to twirl his finger in his curls but pulled his hand down before anyone noticed.

Euphrates signed something to Julian.

Julian translated, "Euphrates says to relax. Peace comes to those who bring it with them."

Maurice turned to Euphrates and nodded his thanks.

Julian continued, "You know the name 'Euphrates' is of Greek origin and roughly translates to 'good, bountiful, fruitful,' and he has certainly brought all those things to Asilomar."

Julian and Euphrates exchanged warms glances of affection. Julian stood up and walked to the end of the patio overlooking the ocean. He added, "We do have one requirement of everyone who stays at Asilomar."

Maurice sat up in an attentive posture upon hearing Julian say the word "requirement." He adjusted his lounge chair to face toward the end of the patio where Julian was.

Julian continued, "There is a reason everyone is here. We ask that you make a commitment, in writing, about why you are here or what your expectations are."

Maurice nodded without saying anything.

"We have a guestbook in the front lobby. When you're ready, we'd like you to sign it and in a few words state why you're here. It's really our only required exercise, and we take it very seriously."

Maurice took a sip of coffee and replied, "Why, yes, I'd be happy to do that. I need to give some thought to exactly how I want to articulate that, but … yes … I'd be honored to sign your guestbook." Maurice had a slight quiver in his voice, realizing he had just committed himself to a longer stay at Asilomar than he had planned. He also had no idea what he would write in the guestbook.

Maurice noticed that Julian had glanced at Claire with a look of anticipation, and that Claire returned an affirmative nod to Julian.

Directing his comments again to Maurice, Julian said, "I spoke with Claire earlier. Since it's her last night and your first full day here, we both thought it might be helpful if she explained her first experience here at Asilomar."

Claire added, "But first let's fill up these wineglasses." She held up her empty glass.

Euphrates retrieved a small bottle of wine and four small glasses from the kitchen. He held it up for everyone to see.

Julian explained, "This is a dessert wine, Maurice. It's called *mistela*, and it is very typical in this region of Spain. It's a sweet wine."

Euphrates poured a little bit in each glass. As he finished serving, Claire tapped her glass, indicating for him to fill it to the top.

Julian chuckled. "We usually only have a small glass of it, but it looks like Claire has other intentions."

"Okay," Claire started, "Julian told me he explained to you how I first met him—in Granada after my husband passed away. Well, that wasn't my real initiation to Asilomar. During that first visit I spent most days grieving and adjusting to losing the man who had been my partner for more than forty years. I returned home to New York soon afterwards."

She took a sip of her *mistela*. "Ooh, this is *so* good." She winked at Euphrates.

She continued, "Well, a little less than a year later, tragedy knocked on my door once again. My only son had moved to Hawaii. We had a little house there, and he was working in the hospitality industry. I received word that he had drowned in a boating accident. Bert was all I had left in terms of immediate family. I traveled from our apartment in New York to the house in Hawaii. I was so devastated that it took weeks before I could even leave the house."

After savoring more wine she added, "One day I was trying to keep busy and was cleaning out my junk drawer—you know, those little drawers in the kitchen where you throw everything you think you'll need to refer to someday but never do? Well, I came across the note that Julian had scribbled down with his phone number, e-mail, and address of Asilomar. I didn't think anything of it at first, except that it reminded me of my first loss, my husband. I put it in the save file. I don't know why, but I did."

Maurice was so attentive to Claire's story that he hadn't yet tried his wine.

"Maurice, try your wine before it evaporates," joked Julian.

Maurice smiled and sampled the wine. "Hmmm, that is good. Almost dessert by itself." The sweetness of the wine made Maurice gently smack his lips together.

Claire took advantage of the pause in storytelling to finish off her wine.

She continued, "Later that day I was on the front porch of the cottage in Hawaii. I suddenly said to myself, 'Claire, you need to snap out of this. You can't die this way.' I got up and looked for that note I put back in the junk drawer. I took it out and left it on the counter for another day, looking at every time I passed. I finally picked it up and decided to contact Julian to see if I could visit. Well, I was on a plane by the end of the week."

Euphrates went around the table and refilled everyone's glass.

Julian remained silent, but his occasional smile and relaxed demeanor indicated he not only was enjoying Claire's recounting of her second visit but was clearly proud of having been able to help her through her challenging time.

Claire took a sip from her refilled glass, being careful not to spill any. "Hmmm, just as good as the first," she joked.

Continuing with her story, she said, "I arrived at Asilomar wondering what I was doing here. It took me no time to feel at home with these gracious and handsome gentlemen here." She gave Euphrates and Julian a salute with her glass, stealing another sip before she placed it back on the table.

"I also became good friends with Fina, as I would walk into town almost every day. I'm addicted to her churros!"

"Okay, Claire," interrupted Julian, "get to the part Maurice is chomping at the bit to hear. Tell him what you signed in the guestbook."

Claire raised her eyebrow and glared at Julian, making fun of his rushing her to tell her story. She continued, "Okay, Okay. Like most everyone else, I waited until the next day to fill in that all-important blank spot in the guestbook. I thought and thought that night. Then I remembered the little sign over the bathroom mirror in the hallway: 'Your dreams are closer than they appear.' Then it hit me. I wrote, 'Dreamless.'"

Claire spoke up again. "I realized I lacked exhilaration. I was missing the spark to ignite me. Yes, there were things I had read about or seen pictures of that I always had thought were fascinating, but I never dreamed of the possibility of ever experiencing them."

Julian interrupted, "You see, Maurice, Claire had invested her entire life and energy in her husband and son. Admirable, yes, but she denied herself her own journey. This is what Asilomar tried to give back to her."

Claire was about to continue her story, but Julian lifted up his hands, as if he wanted to speak. Claire said, "Go ahead, Jules," and motioned with her hand for him to speak.

"Sorry to interrupt, Claire, but you said something I want to comment on. You said you lacked the 'spark.' It didn't take me long to realize that all Claire needed was an experience or two to awaken a desire to experience life again. You know, we all have layers of fantasies buried beneath the baggage, fear, and worries. When you peel back those layers and reach the point where fantasy and reality intersect, it's at this junction where there's a spark, a burst of excitement that moves us forward."

Claire interrupted, giggling. "Yes, I needed a spark but not high voltage! Remember, Julian, you suggested skydiving or parasailing? I thought this man was trying to kill me!"

Julian chuckled. "I think our little adventure on the high seas was enough to give you that boost you were looking for."

Claire continued, "Well, Julian made arrangements at the little harbor in San Felipe to go sailing on an old schooner. Now this wasn't any little sailboat. It looked more like the *Niña*, the *Pinta*, or the *Santa María!*"

"It wasn't that big, Claire." Julian was laughing at Claire's exaggeration.

Claire explained that it might seem surprising that for someone living part-time in Hawaii, she had never really sailed before—just one of those little Sunfish sailboats they rent to tourists. She had expected more people to be on the boat, but it was just her, Julian, Euphrates, and the three-man crew. She described that day as clear and warm, and that the Mediterranean appeared deceptively calm from where they were in the little harbor.

"As soon as the captain motored us out of the harbor, he and his crew started to unroll these huge sails on the two tall masts." Claire held up her arms and waved them over her head as far apart as she could as she was reliving that special day. "They told me to sit down and hold on, and I thought, *Hold on?*"

Julian started to giggle.

"As soon as the first sail was unfurled, I could feel the boat moving forward. After the second mast unfurled, we started to pick up speed. All I remember is that the captain yelled something to the crew. We turned sharply and the boat lunged forward as though a huge propeller had been turned on. The sailboat started to lean. We went faster and faster. I could feel the boat pound against the water as we encountered larger and larger waves. The spray was flying over the deck. Before long I was soaking wet."

Claire was getting a little hoarse from her excited explanation. She stole a quick sip of wine. "At first I held on so tight my knuckles were hurting. But after I realized the boat wasn't going to flip over, I started to absorb what was happening around me: the sensation of speed, the wind, the sound and smell of the spray, the sun sparkling on the water that was running off the deck."

Claire explained that Julian was sitting opposite her, holding onto the slippery railing. He was soaking wet, as well, but he had this huge smile that went from ear to ear. At first she thought he was making fun of her, but then she realized he had created that spark he had just talked about.

"I felt exhilaration on the boat that day. I realized what I had been missing." Claire exhaled and was out of breath from reliving her short adventure.

Maurice noticed that Euphrates was amused, watching Claire's animated account of their sailing adventure.

Julian added, "It was funny. When we got back to the harbor, Claire almost seemed disappointed that it was over. But that evening at dinner she shared a list of places where she thought she might find that same spark. I'd like to think that we made a small breakthrough that day, don't you think, Claire?"

"Definitely. I never did sail again, but I came up with three things I wanted to do after I would go home."

Maurice joked, "Skydiving and parasailing!"

"My dear, those won't ever appear on my list. But I thought of three places I wanted to visit: cruise down the Amazon, go to the midnight baseball game in Fairbanks, Alaska—it's held on the night of the summer solstice—and stay at an inn in Tofino, British Columbia. That part of the Pacific coast gets the brunt of the winter storms, and they can be fierce. Many people go there just to watch the huge waves. Anyway, I've done them all. In fact, I'm going back to Tofino again this winter. Next year I want to see Ayers Rock in Australia, in the outback. It's supposed to be sacred to the aboriginal peoples there."

"Wow!" exclaimed Maurice. "That's terrific."

"Nothing can totally fill the void left by losing my family, but I feel that I have a life of my own that still matters." Claire's face took on a more introspective but content look.

Julian commented, "I never tire of Claire's story. It's so positive and really uncomplicated."

Claire made a final comment. "You know, what I learned most about myself was that when I stayed at home, dreamless, I would begin to feel old and tired. Now I know that as long as I keep in pursuit of something, whether a dream or an adventure, I feel younger and healthier."

Claire held up her near empty glass and toasted everyone.

Julian acknowledged Claire's story by saluting her with his wine goblet. He concluded, "I guess your soul survived the surgery, Claire!"

They all pointed their glasses in Claire's direction and finished off the *mistela*.

Julian suggested, "Hey, no one's finished their dessert yet. Chocolate mousse cheesecake with a persimmon drizzle … brought to you by Chef Euphrates!"

Claire added, "We call persimmons 'kaki' here, Maurice. There's a tree right by my casita."

Maurice commented, "Ah, of course. I've never actually seen them on a tree before." Turning to Euphrates he added, "Sorry, Euphrates, Claire's story was so interesting I forgot all about dessert. It looks fabulous."

Julian signed Maurice's comments to Euphrates, who nodded his acknowledgment. Maurice still felt bad that he wasn't able to communicate directly with Euphrates.

They indulged in their desserts as they watched the sky begin to populate with twinkling stars.

But as Maurice glanced around the patio, he noticed that Julian seemed preoccupied. He had lost the enthusiasm he had during dinner. His eyes were focused downward, and he was caressing his swollen hand.

It was apparent to Maurice that he was masking some anxiety. He could only assume it related to the recent clash with his attackers.

Maurice went back to his casita and sat outside on the steps for a while. He noticed a blue light in a little cage hanging from a tree several yards away. He watched as little bugs and moths were attracted to the magical blue beam, much like how his own daydreams attracted him to imagined journeys to exotic places. For the poor bugs, however, their flights of fantasy ended in the instant of a spark, a flash that illuminated a dismal end to their quest. Unlike these short-lived creatures, he was beginning to see that courageous people can experience successful flights in search of dreams, flights in which the spark illuminates instead of consumes. He wished that one day he would finally put his pen down, signaling the completion of the novel he had dreamed of writing. Until then, he thought, he would keep dreaming.

The next morning Maurice woke up early. He was still feeling some of that Christmas Eve-like excitement from the evening before. Recalling he hadn't seen the rest of the house yet, he was eager to explore more of Asilomar.

He got dressed in loose-fitting jeans, a white T-shirt that had an image of a bear with the word "Bruin" above it, and some white tennis shoes. He opened the front door but felt the coolness of the early morning, so he went back and put on a light hoodie.

As he left his casita, he didn't see anyone around. He didn't walk far before he stopped. The geraniums in the window boxes resumed their brilliant show of red, pink, and salmon. The sweetness of jasmine and orange blossoms had replaced the smell of damp soil and wood that had lingered from the heavy ocean dew. The quiet of the early morning hour was interrupted only by the singing of wild parrots in the fruit trees and the gurgling of a nearby fountain. The grounds were heavily shaded, as the sun was still very low in the sky.

He walked down the path to the house and strolled across the patio to the very edge. The Mediterranean Sea sparkled with a deep-blue fluorescence, as if illuminated from beneath the surface.

Again he felt something rub on his leg. It was Sucre. Maurice knelt down and gave her a big hug. She reciprocated with one of her wet kisses.

After a few more minutes of staring out at the sea, Maurice decided to explore inside the house. He didn't feel entirely comfortable wandering around by himself, but he noticed that the door to the arched hallway was partially open. He thought perhaps Sucre came through that way and it would be okay to go inside.

He walked into the hallway. His eyes didn't have to make much of an adjustment, because the sunlight was still not very bright that early in the morning.

He passed the two arched doorways in the middle of the hallway. He knew the one on the right was the restroom. He assumed the other led to private quarters. He continued past the framed picture on the wall that he had read the day before. He paused to read it again: "If you share a secret, do you think it will alter your destiny?"

After last night's dinner discussion, these words seemed more relevant, although he couldn't yet imagine how sharing his dreams with the Asilomar family might affect his own destiny.

He continued walking down the hallway. There was another picture frame on the wall. It too had a saying written in calligraphy. Maurice whispered it out loud to himself as he read it. "To dream by night is to escape your life. To dream by day is to make it happen." That statement was signed by Stephen Richards.

"Yes, dream with your eyes open," interrupted a voice behind him.

Startled, Maurice turned around. It was Julian. He was wearing a full-length Moroccan tunic.

"Sorry if I startled you. I was just getting up for some coffee. I'm not the early riser that you are apparently."

Equally apologetic, Maurice said, "Oh, I'm sorry if I'm intruding. I'm not sure yet what is private and what is public." From the warmth on his cheeks, he was certain that his face was red from embarrassment, but in the dim hallway he hoped it wasn't noticeable.

"Don't worry. It's impossible to err in this house. If a door is locked, you don't enter. Otherwise, any door may be opened." He patted Maurice on the shoulder. "We'll talk more about 'opening doors'—emotional ones, that is—at some point."

Maurice nodded.

Julian turned and headed back to the kitchen, pausing to say, "Go on, explore. I think Euphrates is up front."

"I will," Maurice answered. He walked cautiously to the end of the hallway. As he neared what he believed was the lobby area, he gently pounded the wall with his fist so he wouldn't startle Euphrates.

As Maurice walked through the little archway into the front area, he saw Euphrates was standing behind the reception desk. Euphrates immediately acknowledged Maurice with a quick sign and nod of the head. He sported a restrained smile and continued to go through the papers on the desk.

Maurice paused and looked slowly around the room. It was a small area. A detailed black iron light fixture hung from the arched ceiling. A bit oversized for such a small room, it looked as though it had once hung in a dining room or library of a larger home. Beyond the desk where Euphrates was working was a curved stairway. He imagined that it led to the turret he had seen on his first day. He hadn't realized that there was a second floor. The stairway was dark, and he decided not to investigate there just yet.

The only other doorway was the main entrance that led to the front gate.

Maurice turned back toward the front desk. Euphrates didn't look up. Behind the desk on the wall was a framed sign. He wasn't able to make it out when they arrived the day before, as their eyes hadn't adjusted to the light. In the same calligraphy as the others down the hall, it read, "Welcome to Asilomar, where the pursuit of dreams begins."

Euphrates finally looked up at Maurice and signaled him to approach. The first thing that caught Maurice's eye was a little sign sitting on the desk. It read, "Español, English, LSE – LSF – ISL. I'm Deaf."

Euphrates tapped Maurice on the shoulder and pointed to a sign on the wall hanging in back of him. It was turned backward facing the wall. He reached and turned the little sign around. It read, "No Miracles Performed Here Today."

Euphrates laughed. Maurice appreciated seeing the lighter side of Euphrates. He thought to himself, *Perhaps Euphrates isn't as indifferent to me as I initially had thought.*

As Maurice started to look away, Euphrates tapped on the desk to get his attention. He pointed to a book lying at the other end of the desk. He motioned for Maurice to come nearer and inspect it. It was bound in a thick chiseled wood cover with a brown leather binding. The design of a flying dragon was embedded in the wood with a rose crystal placed in the middle. Maurice knew from his study of mythology that the dragon sometimes represented a strong force of nature, often of wisdom and strength. The book looked very old, and from its mystical appearance one could almost imagine it to be filled with sorcerers' recipes and spells. The edges of the pages were tipped in gold. There was a lavender ribbon protruding from between the pages.

Euphrates motioned with his hands to open the book.

Maurice gently touched the book's cover, hesitating, as if opening it would release a puff of smoke or a genie. On the very first page, written in the same calligraphy as the pictures in the hallway, were the words "The Guestbook—Asilomar."

Farther down the page, it read, "Welcome to Asilomar. We ask that you register your visit by signing your first name only, the date, and a short reason for your visit."

Maurice looked up at Euphrates, who turned open to the page with the lavender ribbon. He pointed to an empty space labeled "Name" and "Date," pointed to Maurice, and made a scribbling motion with his hand, inviting Maurice to sign.

Next to the book were an old pen and ink bottle. On top of the ornate pen was a carved image of a dragon that was similar to the one on the cover of the guestbook.

Maurice opened the ink bottle and slowly dipped the tip of the pen inside. He shook off the excess ink and signed his first name and the date. At that moment Euphrates raised up his hand, as if to say stop. Then he pointed to the empty space. He shook his head, raised his hand to his temple, and then pointed to put the pen back in its holder.

"He's telling you that you need to wait and really think about what you want to write in that space," said Julian as he appeared from the hallway.

"Oh, thanks, Julian. I wasn't quite sure if I had done something wrong." Maurice looked at Euphrates and nodded his acknowledgment.

"Not at all," reassured Julian. "I think Euphrates recalled from dinner last night that you weren't quite sure how to articulate what you wanted to achieve in this journey."

"He's right, I'm not quite sure yet," confessed Maurice.

"That's fine, but don't wait too long. The sooner you're able to answer that question, the sooner you'll start moving closer to achieving what you want."

"Right," replied Maurice, feeling a little inadequate that he wasn't quite ready to fill in that important space in the book just yet.

"Oh, I meant to tell you yesterday, we usually don't have any formal lunch here. There is food in the refrigerator from dinner last night, or feel free to wander down into town. The same key that opens your casita opens the front door. We leave the gate unlocked during the day."

"Thanks, Julian. I'll probably walk into town with Claire. I need to touch base with Fina anyway about the status of my hotel room in Granada. I guess it's safe to tell them I won't be visiting them?"

Julian grinned and replied, "No, I don't think you will."

Maurice turned and made eye contact with Euphrates and said, "Thank you."

Euphrates again acknowledged him with a modest smile.

"We'll see you at dinner, then, Maurice. Around eight o'clock."

"Great." Maurice walked back down the hall and out to the patio, where he found Claire having coffee.

"Hi. Good morning, Claire. How are you doing? Isn't it a fabulous morning?" Maurice was standing in front of Claire with the sun behind him.

She was chuckling. "It sure looks to be a scorcher of a day too!"

"Scorcher?" Maurice looked puzzled.

"Yeah, the way the sun is lighting up your hair from behind you, it looks like you're already burning up." She laughed. "Seriously, it's cute. I think your hair makes you unique ... and handsome."

"Nice recovery, Claire." Maurice smiled.

"So, did you tour the house a bit? Not much to see really inside, except the guestbook."

Maurice explained, "I saw Euphrates and Julian up front. They explained the guestbook to me. Guess I'm not ready for that important moment yet."

"You mean your entry?" Claire confirmed.

Maurice nodded.

"That's fine. It's better that you think through it a bit. Not that it's like a legal document or anything, but Julian will base a lot of his interaction with you based on what you say."

"I think I'm close, but I want to sleep on it. Say, are we going into town this morning? I want to check with Fina to make sure my hotel and everything has been taken care of."

"Sure, as soon as I finish up here, we can go. We can stop by and visit Euphrates later too," Claire added.

"Visit him? Where?" asked Maurice with great interest.

"Well, a few times a week he opens a little booth in the plaza selling good luck charms to tourists. He supplements the salary he gets from Julian for helping at Asilomar, like taking care of the garden, and of course, those fabulous dinners." She giggled. "Funny, Julian doesn't believe in those charms. I'm not so sure about Euphrates, but he does wear one around his neck. Good advertising, I guess!" Claire let out a little laugh.

Maurice asked Claire, "How long are you going to be staying here this trip?"

"I'm actually leaving tomorrow. This was just a short trip. As I mentioned in the car, I had been on a cruise that ended in Lisbon, and since I was relatively close, I decided to drive here for a quick visit. I have to go home to settle some property issues soon, but we'll exchange contact information. I like staying in touch with my Asilomar family."

"For sure!" Maurice said. "But I'm sorry you're leaving so soon."

Claire finished her coffee and sweet roll, and the two headed down the hill to town. The walk down seemed a lot shorter.

When they got to the bakery, Fina was out front washing down the steps.

"*Hola*. What a pair you guys make, huffing and puffing!"

Maurice laughed and said, "Hey, I don't see you running up that hill."

Fina responded, "I've done my share of going up there, *hijo*." She slapped her thighs to show off her strong legs.

"Fina, do I need to call the hotel, or has everything been settled with them? It looks like Asilomar will be my home for a while," he explained.

"Don't worry, I told them you won't be coming for a while. They aren't charging you anything."

"Thanks, I appreciate your handling it. My Spanish isn't that dependable, especially on the telephone."

Fina invited them in for a cup of coffee. Maurice joked that he had had more caffeine in the last forty-eight hours than in the previous forty-eight days.

After they chatted for a while, Claire told Fina she was going to take Maurice on a tour around the town.

"Well, that won't take but a few minutes." Fina's whole body seemed to shake when she chuckled.

They finished their coffee, and Claire led Maurice down the little winding street. As they walked, Maurice stumbled on one of the cobblestones and almost fell.

Claire said, "You gotta watch where you're walking around here. These streets are rough, and sometimes it's difficult to see the potholes. Experience was a cruel teacher for me."

In a few short minutes they entered a small plaza. In the middle there were three very tall and elegant palm trees with their trunks painted white. Surrounding the plaza were two-story whitewashed buildings. The first floors were occupied by businesses, mainly cafés, restaurants, and souvenir shops.

Claire announced, "This is downtown San Felipe."

Maurice smiled. "I guess Fina was right. It didn't take long to walk through town."

Maurice followed Claire across the plaza to a bright-colored canopy. Underneath was a table that had an attractive display of trinkets. Euphrates was sitting under the shaded tent, reading. It was early, and there weren't many visitors in town yet.

Claire walked up to the table. Euphrates didn't look up at first, but after a moment he must have sensed someone was standing there.

He jumped up, and with a big grin spreading across his handsome face he hugged Claire and gave her a kiss on each cheek.

Maurice turned to Claire. "I always liked that custom of two kisses."

Claire chuckled. "But never on the first meeting!" They both laughed.

As Maurice extended his hand, Euphrates grasped it with both of his hands and gave it a firm shake. Little beads of perspiration glistened in the bright sunlight like crystals on Euphrates's youthful face.

"Hi, Euphrates," said Maurice. "Pretty," he added as he pointed to the shiny items laid out on the table that was covered by a silky Moroccan tapestry.

Euphrates cocked his head to the side and raised his hands to his sides, palms up, as if saying, "It's okay. It keeps me busy."

Maurice scanned the table, expecting typical tourist stuff that would find its way to someone's junk drawer within a week of returning home. He was surprised to find a unique selection of artistically crafted items made of what may have been silver. Others were ceramic. Also on the table was the same sign that was on the desk at Asilomar. It read, "Español, English, LSE – LSF – ISL. I'm Deaf."

Maurice reached over the table and picked up one of the objects. It was an image of a stick man standing with legs apart and arms outstretched above him. The figure was holding an arc. Euphrates handed Maurice a postcard that explained the meaning and origin of the figure, which was represented in various forms, such as pins, charms, wall hangings, and even wine bottle stoppers.

It read, "INDALO MAN is a prehistoric symbol found in the cave of Los Letreros in the region of Andalucia, Spain. Dating over 4,000 years, it has become a symbol of good luck."

Claire said, "These are very popular here. You'll see that symbol everywhere you go. It's a symbol used by the entire province. Many believe the man is holding a rainbow."

Symbol art created by Shara Gardner

Maurice gently put the Indalo Man back and noticed another type of charm on the other end of the table.

After studying it a bit closer, he noticed that it was in the shape of a hand, fingers together but the palm open. Like the Indalo Man, the symbol took various forms. Some were decorated with additional adornment such as precious stones, while others were quite plain. The theme was repeated on items, such as earrings, charms for necklaces, bracelets, and larger ones that could be mounted on a wall.

Euphrates reached over the table and handed him another postcard. It read, "A HAMSA, or Hand of Fatima, is an ancient talisman against the 'evil eye.' It has also become a symbol of good fortune. Fatima was a daughter of the prophet Mohammed. Various versions of the Hamsa are recognized in many cultures and religions including Judaism, Buddhism, Christianity, and Islam."

When Maurice looked back up, Euphrates reached into the neck of his shirt and pulled out the chain that was around his neck. At first, Maurice's attention was drawn to the dark curls of black hair on his chest. Maurice worried that Euphrates may notice him staring at him, so he turned away.

Symbol art created by Shara Gardner

He leaned forward facing Maurice so he could show him the charm on the end of his chain. It was a small hamsa with an amber-colored stone in the middle of the hand.

The subtle smell of sweet incense already had alerted Maurice's senses.

"That's beautiful. Very artistic," he said, hoping that Euphrates would be able to read his lips.

Stretching her arm toward Maurice and dangling her bracelet in front of him, Claire added proudly, "I have a hamsa charm on my bracelet. See? I like that it crosses many cultures and religions of the Mideast."

Maurice was impressed with the hamsa, as well, especially for its history and universal appeal across cultures.

Claire leaned closer to Maurice and gently held his arm. She said in a soft voice so no one else could hear, "I think that Euphrates's exotic look helps to attract visitors' interest in these talisman objects. Like me, perhaps they attach their own spiritual value to them—whether a memory of here, an adventure they had, or one they want to have."

Maurice listened and nodded, thinking to himself that Euphrates gave him that same feeling and more.

Claire added, "I relate certain feelings and emotions to the charm on my bracelet. Certainly nothing to do with the charm's original intention, but when I glance at it I'm reminded of Asilomar wherever I happen to be. You know, Euphrates makes many of the more intricate hamsa talismans. He's quite artistic."

Maurice agreed. "Yes, he's very talented to produce those designs. I'm very impressed."

Claire tugged on his shirt. "Let's walk around a little more. I'd like to show you the beach, and then we should probably get a little lunch before we head back up the hill." She signaled to Euphrates if he wanted to join them, but he reached down and held up a little bag that held the snack he had brought with him.

Claire and Euphrates hugged and exchanged kisses once more. Maurice was about to extend his hand when Euphrates surprised him by walking to the end of the table to give him a friendly hug.

As they started to walk across the plaza, Maurice said to Claire, "Gosh, Euphrates seemed much friendlier today."

Claire turned and gave him a wink. "Maybe it will be a kiss next time."

He was embarrassed by Claire's bold comment, but he did feel a growing infatuation with this mysterious man. As they crossed the plaza, he looked back at Euphrates, who was already busy with the first arriving tourists. He saw Euphrates briefly return his glance.

Claire and Maurice walked another block. Maurice already could see the ocean and was eager to put his feet in the Mediterranean for the first time. They came upon a colorfully tiled boardwalk that paralleled the beach for about two hundred yards. On one side were cafés and a few small hotels. On the other side the beach stretched about one hundred yards out to the water. The tiles adorning the boardwalk were placed in geometric patterns with an occasional tiled image of the Indalo Man.

"See what I mean?" Claire chuckled as she pointed to the tile image. "You'll find him everywhere." They walked to the middle of the boardwalk. Heading out over the beach toward the water was a wooden walkway just wide enough for two. Claire steered Maurice to the walkway. An occasional plank was missing, so they had to walk carefully.

The boardwalk ended just yards from the water's edge. Maurice rolled up his jeans and took off his shoes and socks. Walking into the relatively calm water, his whole body relaxed as he wiggled his feet into the wet sand. He yelled to Claire, "Oh, does this ever feel good. The water is warm, and it's so clear."

Claire waved him on to take a walk along the beach. She sat down at the edge of the wooden walkway and watched the few tourists who were walking by. It wasn't vacation season, so beaches were relatively empty of visitors.

Maurice walked slowly toward the water's edge, just far enough to where the breaking waves would wash up over his ankles. In both directions the beach disappeared into rocky cliffs that reached out into the sea. He slowly made his way from one end to another and back again. As he came back to where Claire was sitting, he paused and turned facing out to the sea. He didn't want his little excursion to end but promised himself he would come back again. At one end of the beach he noticed a small restaurant whose patio extended out to the sand. He knew he wanted to return one day and enjoy a peaceful lunch by the sea.

Maurice finally rejoined Claire.

"Did you have a nice walk?" Claire asked.

"Ah, I love the ocean. I could have walked back and forth all day." Maurice sighed.

Claire laughed. "I almost thought you were going to!"

Maurice looked at his watch. "Oh, Claire, I'm sorry. I didn't realize I was out there so long."

An hour had almost passed while he made his trips up and down the beach.

"No worries, I was enjoying my time too. There's nothing like the ocean to settle one's thoughts, is there?" she added.

"You're so right. This is just wonderful. I have to come back and spend some time here. I bet it's especially nice early in the morning too." Maurice had taken off his shirt. He noticed Claire eyeing him and then nodded in the direction of a young lady sunbathing.

"She's been checking you out. I probably should get you home before the ladies rush you," Claire joked. She knew better.

"Ha-ha. You don't have to worry about that." Maurice smirked.

Maurice looked down at himself, thinking he still had his tight physique from his wrestling days. The sun reflected off the reddish hair on his chest that ran down in a line and disappeared into his jeans.

He put his shoes and socks back on, and they walked back

through town, waving to Euphrates as they passed through the plaza. His booth was surrounded by people checking out his wares.

They stopped at a little café and enjoyed some tapas and a glass of wine. When the waiter asked for the order, Maurice didn't hesitate. "Anchovies, ham, and cheese, please."

Afterward they stopped by Fina's to say hello before they made the trek up the hill, but she had closed for siesta. Claire commented that she never really rested but instead was probably upstairs watching a *novela* on TV. She didn't want to disturb her.

They made their slow climb up the hill until they came to the big wooden gates.

"Not sure I want to take that hike every day," said Claire, whose heavy breathing and flushed face were testaments to the demanding climb up the hill.

"But it's great exercise," said Maurice and clowned, flexing his biceps.

Maurice pushed open one of the heavy gates, and they walked up to the front door.

Maurice took out his key. It took a little effort, but he wiggled it and heard the lock make a clicking sound. He pushed the door open, and they both let out a sigh.

"It seems strange that Julian doesn't lock the gate, doesn't it?"

"Yes, it is," remarked Claire as she shook her head. "I've told him many times that he needs to start locking it, especially in light of those hoodlums who are after him. But he's stubborn. He says he doesn't want to feel like his house is a prison."

The house was quiet. They walked through the hall, across the patio, and out to the casitas. The hibiscus bushes basked in the bright sunlight, showing off their yellow, red, and pink flowers that were the size of dinner plates.

Maurice said, "I'll see you at dinner."

They walked to their respective casitas.

As soon as Maurice got settled, he sat up on the bed. Although he was a bit tired, he pulled out his laptop computer and started writing notes. He thought to himself, *I have a lot of catching up to do.*

It seemed like no time had passed when the dinner chime rang. Maurice had fallen asleep with the computer on his lap. He jumped up, splashed water on his face, put on a clean shirt, and rushed out to the patio.

When he got to the dinner table, Claire was already seated.

"Oversleep, honey? I had a good nap myself."

"Gosh, I'm not sure." Maurice laughed. "I spent a good part of the afternoon writing, but I guess I dozed off. Don't know how long I was out."

Claire asked, "Are you happy with what you've written so far?"

Maurice was always private about his writing and gave Claire the same answer he had given little Calvin on the plane. "It's just notes, impressions, you know. Nothing special."

Claire argued, "Maurice, it's all special. Someday it will all come together; you'll see."

Maurice appreciated Claire's positive comments and gave her shoulder a soft squeeze.

Claire joked, "I bet you could break nuts with those big hands."

Maurice responded by playfully punching one hand with his fist.

Just then Euphrates and Julian came out from the kitchen, each carrying a big tray.

Euphrates waved with his one free hand, set his tray down, and returned to the kitchen. The tray had a basket of bread and a cooled bottle of white wine with condensation dripping down the side.

Julian's tray had a huge bowl of steaming red prawns and a smaller bowl of lemon wedges.

"Hello, guys," said Julian as he went over and gave Claire a kiss on each cheek. He walked behind Maurice and placed his hands on Maurice's shoulders. "How was your day? Did you get the cook's tour of San Felipe, Maurice?"

"Ah, yes, we had a nice time. We stopped and saw Euphrates's kiosk. He seemed to be doing a brisk business by the time we left."

Julian commented, "He does surprisingly well. It's good for him too. He gets out of the house for a while and makes a pretty good side income from it."

Maurice continued, "We walked down to the beach too. Man, the ocean is so wonderful here. Like Claire said, it's very relaxing to look out at the open expanse of blue … and very productive for a daydreamer like me!"

"Ha, you're so right. That's part of what makes Asilomar so special, I think," added Julian. "One of these days I'll ask Euphrates to take you down to our beach. Well, it's not *our* beach, but you can access it only by climbing down a steep path on the other side of the patio."

Euphrates returned with a large bowl of salad, which consisted simply of fresh greens, sliced tomatoes, avocados, and a little red onion. He made a final trip to the kitchen and brought out a round pan that looked like it would contain pizza. The dish was sliced in wedges.

Julian explained, "This is a *patata frita*, fried potatoes and eggs—a common dish here."

Pointing to the prawns, he added, "And this part of the Mediterranean is famous for these large shrimp."

Julian directed his explanation to Maurice, since Claire was already familiar with the dishes.

"It all looks delicious," commented Maurice.

Euphrates poured the wine.

Holding up his glass, Julian recited the same toast as the previous evening. "May your journeys be long, and may your dreams be forever. *Salud.*"

There was a chorus of "*Saluds*" around the table as they clinked their glasses.

"Hmmm, this is a delightful wine," said Claire as she took a long sip. "I guess by now, Maurice, you know I like my wine." She giggled.

Julian raised his hand toward Euphrates. "Pacha discovered it last spring. It's from a local vineyard on the other side of the mountain. It's nice and dry, isn't it? Perfect with seafood, I think."

Euphrates nodded and pointed to the red prawns that were still steaming.

They passed around the different bowls of food and started to eat. Maurice was uncertain how to negotiate eating the whole prawns but watched Euphrates and Julian and followed their lead.

"Claire, are you going directly back to New York?" asked Julian.

"No," said Claire. "I'm off to Hawaii first to settle that property with the lawyers. Then I'm going to fly to British Columbia, Canada, and back to Tofino." She explained to Maurice, "I want to get there in time for the stormy season in the north Pacific. It's sort of my little Asilomar away from home."

"My gosh, you seem to be always on the go and doing exciting things," observed Maurice.

Claire joked, "Well, it's not the *vida loca*, but I am *loca* for *la vida!*"

That brought laughter from all around the table.

Claire continued, "And remember what I said about how I feel younger and invigorated when I am adventuring. Like a famous lady chef once said, 'Everything in moderation, including moderation.'" Claire asked, "Maurice, have you given more thought to what you want to write in the guestbook?"

"You know, I've been thinking a lot about it. I'm not sure if it's appropriate but—"

Julian interrupted, "Nothing is inappropriate as long as it's positive, personal to you, and harmful to no one."

Claire added, "And of course, there's never a guarantee you're going to live up to what you write. It doesn't come without a lot of effort, right, Julian?"

Maurice took several sips of wine as he listened.

"Claire's right. It merely is putting a stake in the ground. It takes a lot of effort, self-examination—a process that can be painful, as well as rewarding."

Claire chuckled out loud. "Oh my, and there have been some folks that have come here expecting miracles." Looking at Julian, she continued, "Remember the lady who was desperate to achieve immortality so she could host another millennium New Year's Eve party in 2099?"

Julian shook his head.

"Dr. Freud to the white courtesy phone!" mimicked Claire playfully.

Maurice and Claire laughed.

Maurice thought, *Ah, that's why Euphrates had that silly sign behind the desk: "No miracles performed today."*

Julian replied, "Yes, we've had some very troubled people come to us, some who need professional care—much more than we can provide. We can only help to unlock what's already there."

"But back to you, Maurice. You said you've given your guestbook entry some more thought?"

All eyes were again focused on Maurice, who started to feel self-conscious. He quickly ran his hand through his hair and looked up at Julian and then across to Euphrates.

"Let me ask you a question first, Julian." Maurice squirmed with discomfort. He continued, "Well, in the hallway I noticed in a frame there was a saying—I can't remember the author's name. I think he was of Arab descent. Anyway, I can't remember his exact words, but he asked the question, 'Do you think your destiny could be altered by disclosing your secret desires to others?'" Maurice looked directly at Julian and asked, "Do you think this is true?"

Julian didn't hesitate in his answer. "Maurice, one of the reasons that this particular quote is on the wall is that I do believe it is true. And it can work two ways." Maurice noticed that Claire had his undivided attention. Apparently, in all her visits the quote never resonated with her. "Each of our lives has multiple endings depending on the critical path-changing decisions we either consciously make or the ones the universe makes for us."

Continuing his explanation, Julian explained, "If you share a secret or dream with someone who openly doubts your ability or cynically questions the possibility of achieving something, then that negative interference usually has a restraining effect on your pursuit of that goal. But, if that person is supportive and creates a positive and reinforcing environment, then yes, that person's destiny could be altered with the increased likelihood of him or her achieving that dream."

Julian added, "Very often family, close friends, and coworkers are not as supportive as we would like to think. It's important to choose carefully with whom you are going to share your dreams and aspirations."

Maurice made a passing glance around the entire table before describing what he felt was a somewhat embarrassing guestbook entry.

He said in a soft voice, "Freedom and courage to live and write." Maurice immediately took a sip of wine and waited for the others' reactions with considerable anxiety.

Julian quickly signed Maurice's statement to Euphrates.

For Maurice, the silence at the table lasted an eternity. Julian and Euphrates looked at one another and then smiled.

"That's a very lofty but attainable dream, Maurice. But your statement involves more than just writing." Julian drank his wine with a thoughtful look on his face. "Freedom and courage," he repeated. "That implies there's something that's keeping you from living as you would like, and something discouraging you from writing. There's something that's holding you back. Am I right?"

"Well, yeah," confessed Maurice.

Maurice noticed Euphrates and Claire had already started eating the prawns.

He thought for a moment and continued. "I daydream all the time. I've got that part down to a science. I continually write down observations of my surroundings and fantasize what it would be like to feel the exhilaration of discovery and adventure that Claire talked about. But I don't permit myself to actually experience and feel those emotions. My dreams are just that—dreams."

Maurice twirled his hair with his fingers. He hadn't yet grasped what his unplanned visit to Asilomar would mean to him.

He continued, "Claire, I envy your fearless quest for adventure."

Claire interrupted, "Maurice, being adventurous has nothing to do with being fearless. I've felt fear and uncertainty about many of the experiences I've created for myself. This is normal. But what makes the reward so great is not just the adventure but the satisfaction of overcoming those fears. Remember, I said that these were experiences that I created. You can't wait for them to come and find you. I still look for those adventures that may put me outside my comfort level. You don't have to live without a net, but I certainly have my limits. That skydiving thing … forget it!"

Maurice commented, "You're just so positive … living as though life will never end." Maurice put some prawns on his plate but wasn't yet sure how to eat them.

Claire laughed. "Sweetie, I'm not trying to escape mortality. I'm just trying to race it to the finish line, and I think you're a bit of a worry wart, Maurice."

Maurice smiled and nodded. "Yeah, I guess worry does walk at my side."

Claire continued, "Ha! You make me think of Mark Twain. He said, 'I've been through a lot of horrible stuff in my life, and some of it actually happened.'"

Maurice and Julian laughed.

Claire took a sip of wine and added, "Look, consider this very trip you've decided to take. You made that choice. You have already moved outside your comfort level by being willing to change your itinerary and remain at Asilomar, even though we may have given you a bit of a nudge. But you're here." Claire ended her sermon with a giggle.

Maurice was overwhelmed by the frank discussion, and as anxious as he was, he felt pleased with himself for having been willing to share his self-examination with the others.

"Are you feeling vulnerable right now, Maurice?" Julian asked.

"Yeah, sorta, I guess." He looked at Claire and asked with a tentative smile, "So, is this what you call 'open soul surgery'?"

"It's definitely a start, my dear." Claire reached across the table and gave his hand a squeeze.

Julian gave Maurice a nod of encouragement and asked, "What else, Maurice?"

Maurice was a little surprised by Julian's follow-up question, hoping that his "surgery" was over for the evening.

Maurice thought for a moment and continued, "Lack of confidence. I'm not sure I'm a good enough writer. I've only written business articles. I guess I'm afraid of trying and failing. I write lots of notes, but I'm not sure what they all mean. That lightbulb of inspiration hasn't lit up yet, and I don't know how to turn it on."

Julian set his wineglass on the table and put his hands, palms up, next to it. "See, my friend, you are in the right place. We'll help you work on those very things, although your acknowledgment of them is more than half the battle. Right now I think you're in a place of chaos and confusion. I think your experiences here will spark your imagination. That will help to restore some order out of the chaos and instill hope and confidence. I truly believe that."

Euphrates tapped on the table to get Maurice's attention. He raised his wineglass in his direction.

"Thank you both. That means a lot," replied Maurice, who still wasn't completely sure why he was there and why Julian had taken an interest in him. He sighed and took a slow sip of his wine.

"What kind of novel do you want to write, or aren't you sure of that quite yet?" Julian inquired.

"No, I'm not really sure. My journal of notes is a miscellaneous collection of observations and impressions. I'm hoping that eventually it will all lead somewhere." Maurice knew his answer was rather vague, but he was being honest.

"You have to start somewhere, Maurice. I really think some of your experiences here at Asilomar will help you to organize some of your thoughts. We'll make sure of that."

Maurice shifted uncomfortably in his chair.

Julian went on to say, "We teach ourselves how to succeed and how to fail, Maurice. If you worry all the time, then each day you're teaching yourself how to worry better. For every moment you're happy, you're learning how to be even happier. For every time you believe you can write a novel, you will get closer to seeing that lightbulb burst into brightness."

After a pause in conversation, they resumed eating their dinner.

Maurice was still struggling with peeling his prawns. He looked over at Euphrates, who proceeded to give him a quick demonstration. They were whole shrimps with shell, head, and legs still intact. He struggled at first, but once Maurice got the technique of opening them up down the middle to peel away the soft shell, he was able to catch up with the rest.

Dessert was another impressive creation by Euphrates—a lemon and guava torte, accompanied by the mandatory espresso.

It was a quiet evening after dinner. There was little conversation. Julian seemed to be in a thoughtful mood, sitting off to the side. Claire had brought some knitting, and Euphrates was in the kitchen cleaning up. Maurice offered to help, but Euphrates motioned for him to sit and relax. For several moments Maurice watched Claire. She had put on a pair of glasses as she prepared to start her knitting. He started to chuckle. He thought, *Here's a seventy-year-old lady who think and acts like a woman half of her age, who likes to be thought of as hip and ready for action. Yet she puts on these outrageous pink beaded glasses with rhinestones on either side of the pointed frames. Something a drag queen would wear.*

Peering over her glasses, she asked, "What's going on over there, Maurice? Did I miss something?"

"Busted," he confessed. "I'm sorry, Claire, but those glasses are from a time warp."

"I figured that was it. I usually get that reaction. Restores my faith that people are still watching. Hee hee!"

Maurice shook his head, laughing, and left Claire to her knitting. He walked out to the edge of the patio and sat on top of the stucco wall facing the ocean.

He could see ships in the distance, their lights flickering on the darkening horizon. He zipped up his hoodie, as the breeze was getting cool, but he didn't want the evening to end just yet. He was proud of himself for having taken the opportunity to self-examine. He appreciated the safe environment created by Julian, Euphrates, and Claire. He felt an overwhelming sense of home that he couldn't really explain. He didn't attempt to understand it, but he knew he wanted to keep feeling whatever it was that he was feeling.

⌒⬥⌒

Maurice didn't sleep quite as well that night. He wasn't sure if it was the heavy dinner and wine, being overtired from all the activity during the day, or subconsciously thinking about the commitment he was making at Asilomar.

He got out of bed several times to sit on the front step of his casita. He would stare at the garden and occasionally jot down some notes on his iPad.

He finally dozed off, awakening to a clipping sound. The sun was already filling up his room with an orange glow. He got out of bed and looked out the window. In front of the empty casita next to his he saw Euphrates. He was shirtless, trimming the overgrown bushes and bundling them up in a large canvas sack.

Tall and slight of build, he still was much more athletic-looking than what Maurice had imagined under the loose-fitting garments that he had been wearing. His arms were long and taught, and as he turned around Maurice noticed his chest was covered in a pattern of dark hair that followed the curves of his chest and stomach.

Very sexy, Maurice thought. He quickly closed the window shutter and tried to shift his thoughts to something else. *The last thing you need to do is to complicate your stay here, Dumbo.* He silently scolded himself for letting his imagination take a quick trip to a physical and sexual place. He didn't take this vacation to look for romantic trysts, let alone to find a boyfriend. He hadn't had much luck the past few years in the romance department and had all but given up on finding a long-term relationship. He often faulted himself for lack of commitment but knew that he had made some bad choices in men, as well.

Maurice showered and put on jeans and a fresh T-shirt. His stomach was growling, and he hoped there would be coffee and rolls out for breakfast. As he left the casita, Euphrates had moved and was working by a casita farther away. Maurice waved as Euphrates glanced in his direction. Euphrates lifted up his arm and waved back. The silver chain around his neck sparkled in the sunlight. Maurice thought of going over to say hello but then decided it would be awkward not being able to communicate. What would he say? He'd probably look stupid, especially since he'd more than likely find himself staring at Euphrates's shirtless body. He decided to head straight to the patio in search of breakfast.

Maurice was alone on the patio. He was surprised as he fully expected early bird Claire to be on her second croissant already. Actually, he rather enjoyed having the patio to himself for a little while.

Instead of sitting at the table, he plopped down on one of the cozy lounges closest to the edge of the patio. He sat low in the chair, staring up at the sky. The sun felt warm and comforting. An occasional puffy white cloud would pass overhead, momentarily blocking the sun's warm rays. During those moments he felt the influence of the cooler ocean air. He thought the alternating sensations—the warmth, then the coolness, and the returning warmth—reminded him of the emotional roller coaster that he had been riding the last couple of days—exuberant with the joy of discovery of Asilomar, anxious about stepping outside of his comfort level, and then reassured by the sincerity of Julian and Euphrates.

"Good morning, dear." Claire's greeting broke his brief meditation.

Maurice looked around. "Hi, Claire. I beat you this morning."

"I was busy packing. Heading home this morning, you know. I'm always sad about leaving." Claire shook her head. "I always worry this will be my last visit here, but I guess Asilomar has blessed me with more than my share of good 'soul surgery.'"

Maurice joined her at the table. He hadn't noticed but Euphrates had returned to the house while he was lounging. As soon as he and Claire sat down, Euphrates came out of the kitchen with coffee and rolls. With his floor-length tunic blowing in the breeze, he made his usual stop by Claire to give her a kiss on each cheek. He extended both arms to shake Maurice's hand. This time Maurice noticed that Euphrates's grip was firmer and longer-lasting than before.

Euphrates disappeared into the kitchen.

Maurice turned to Claire. "Claire, I have a question for you before you leave. I don't like to pry, but yesterday when we were at Fina's you talked about Julian's son. It must be hard for him not to have him living up here with him."

The serious look that overtook Claire couldn't be mistaken. "Yes, it causes him a great deal of stress. He's cut back on the number of visitors to Asilomar too, wanting to spend more private time with little Julian. He visits Fina every couple of days and takes little Julian out to the beach or for a ride. Fina usually spends the weekends here at Asilomar. Even then, he is always watchful of strangers."

"That must be hard," replied Maurice. "I certainly understand the sensitivity, but I appreciate you sharing that with me."

"Yes, it's very stressful for Julian. He will do anything to protect his little boy. That's all that's important to him. Asilomar isn't the driving force in his life anymore."

At that moment, Julian walked out, with Sucre in tow close behind. "Good morning, all."

"Good morning, Julian," greeted Maurice, still thinking about what Claire had just told him.

"Hello, Jules. I'm all packed up. You know how I hate to leave!" Putting on a strong face, she continued, "I was telling Maurice I never know if it will be my last visit." Claire looked up at Julian with a forced smile, obviously trying to hide her sadness about leaving. Julian planted a kiss on each cheek.

It was the first time Maurice had actually seen Claire with a sad face and lacking her usual upbeat energy.

Julian admonished, "I think you'll be back, Claire. The universe isn't done with you quite yet." He chuckled.

The contemplative look remained on Claire's wrinkled face. "Knowing what I know now, I wish I had another lifetime, but we only get one. That's why I don't rest."

Maurice and Julian were silent and listened to Claire, as though she was the old and wise sage, which she had indeed become.

Claire continued, "Funny, many of us don't get the wisdom of how to live well until later in life. Perhaps it makes the experience more intense and more meaningful."

Julian hesitated and then added, "Claire, while that's true for many of us, I hope that both Maurice and Euphrates will learn from you and come to that conclusion much sooner."

Claire gave both Maurice and Euphrates a thumbs-up and finally broke a smile. Julian asked Claire, "You said your flight was at noon, right? Euphrates will take the jeep and drive you to Almería Airport. He'll still be able to make it back in time to open his booth on the plaza."

Claire nodded in appreciation and left the table to get her things together.

Euphrates cleared the table, leaving Julian and Maurice alone.

"What are your plans today, Maurice?" asked Julian.

Maurice really hadn't thought through his day yet but responded, "I think I'll just spend a day relaxing. I might head into town and visit the beach again. I feel like I have a lot of thinking to do today, you know what I mean?"

Julian laughed. "Yes, I know what you mean."

Maurice offered, "If there's anything I can do around the house or garden to help out, let me know. I like to keep busy too."

"I appreciate that. I think we're good, but I'll keep that in mind." Julian winked and sipped the coffee he brought out with him.

"I've got some paperwork I need to work on this morning

and then get preparations for dinner started." Julian got up and gave Maurice a warm slap on the back. "Let me know if you need anything, okay?"

Maurice was again alone. He walked to the edge of the patio and sat on the wall, looking out of the expanse of water below. He was so mesmerized by the expanse of blue that he hadn't realized nearly twenty minutes had passed. There was a tap on his shoulder.

"Dear, I just want to say good-bye." Claire gave Maurice a big kiss on his cheek. "I want to thank you again for being my knight in shining armor. I know you'll be glad it worked out this way."

Maurice was touched. He gave her a big hug. "I'm so glad we met, Claire. There just may be one day when I look back and say I owe it all to you."

"Honey, yes, you will owe it all to me!" Claire reached up and rubbed his curly red locks. "By the way, I left a note on your door with all my contact information—Facebook, e-mail, phone, address … the whole works. Please do let me know how you're doing. I mean it."

Maurice gave Claire one more farewell hug and a kiss on each cheek.

"Ooh, you're learning quickly!" Claire started to leave but then stopped and came back to whisper something in Maurice's ear.

"Just remember, your dreams are hiding in full view. Dream with your eyes wide open."

Maurice watched as she and Euphrates disappeared down the hallway.

He sat on the patio wall for a few minutes, looking out over the expanse of blue ocean. As he sat there, he remembered that little restaurant he saw on the beach. He decided to dash into town for lunch, since everyone else was busy.

After hiking down the hill, he walked across the plaza in town and headed directly to the beach. It was a very quiet day with few people around. The weather was eerily still. The ocean was like glass except for occasional breaking waves. The sun would peak through the passing clouds, creating a patchwork of reflections on the ocean surface.

Maurice entered the restaurant and asked to have one of the tables close to the water. There were only three other customers, but they were eating inside. He was happy to have the outdoor patio to himself and pulled a chair around the small table so he could face out to the sea. After he ordered several tapas, the waiter brought him a basket of fresh bread and a glass of white wine. Pausing a moment to absorb the idyllic setting, he put the wineglass to his lips and tasted the wine. He exhaled. *Perfect*, he thought, *I'm having my Shirley Valentine moment.* Shirley Valentine was a character in the 1980s movie who left her controlling husband and predictable life as a London housewife to experience an unscripted adventure in Greece.

Maurice sat hypnotized by the peaceful setting by the sea. Like Shirley in the movie, he had become infatuated by the beauty of Asilomar, encouraged by the free spirits of his new friends, excited by the new possibilities that he was just now beginning to understand, and, most of all, liberated from some of the fears and doubts that had held him back for so long.

It wasn't all perfectly clear to him yet, but he felt that something special was happening to him. The feeling reminded him of an article he had read about *saudade*, a word of Portuguese origin that had no direct translation, but it's been described as a feeling of nostalgia for something that may not have even happened yet. Portuguese writer Manuel de Melo described it as "a pleasure you suffer, an ailment you enjoy."

Maurice was enjoying his moment of *saudade* and didn't want it to end. After he finished his second glass of wine, he realized he had been sitting there for over an hour.

Time to head back, he told himself. He took one last look out to the ocean before he went inside to pay his bill. He walked slowly back through town, savoring his peaceful midday excursion.

Once back at Asilomar, Maurice returned to the comfortable lounge chair on the patio. He snuggled deep into the soft cushion so he could again enjoy the view of the passing clouds overhead.

He reviewed his day at the beach and daydreamed about writing in Asilomar's lush gardens and enjoying future evenings on the patio. The disappointment about Claire's sad departure was replaced by a quiet excitement. He drifted off to sleep.

Eyes Wide Open

A loud crash woke Maurice up from his nap on the patio. Then there was another crash, glass breaking, and the crack of wood splintering. He heard a loud grunt, followed by the distressed voices of two men yelling.

Even though they were speaking a language he didn't recognize, the threatening and aggressive nature of the speech was obvious.

Maurice was still groggy and at first thought he was having a bad dream. He got up and looked toward the house.

The kitchen door to the patio was shut, but he was certain the commotion was coming from inside.

Through the window he saw the silhouettes of two figures struggling. It was Julian. His assailant had both hands clenched around his throat, but he was wrestling with his aggressor to attempt to free himself.

Without deliberating, Maurice jumped off the lounge and pulled the kitchen door open so hard it almost came off its hinges. His sudden rush of adrenaline propelled him toward the battling men.

He had no time to think other than knowing instinctually that he had to free Julian before he choked to death.

As he grabbed the attacker from behind, he wrapped his strong forearms across the man's neck. The attacker was taller than Maurice, but Maurice was stronger and had the advantage of two free hands.

He tightened his grip and at the same time used his legs to pull one of the attacker's legs out from under him. As Maurice pulled his neck back, the man's grip loosened and Julian slumped to the floor. With his arms now free, the attacker wiggled free of Maurice and quickly turned around, knocking him to the floor. Together they rolled across the floor, and Maurice felt his back slam into the kitchen cabinets. The man landed a punch to Maurice's chin, and he felt his head spin for a second. The assailant grabbed a kitchen knife off the counter and lunged toward Maurice, who tried to deflect his attack. He felt a swipe of the knife across his stomach, but his adrenaline masked any sensation of pain. Using one of his old wrestling moves, he grabbed one of the man's arms and bent it back to where he yelled.

Maurice rolled over on top of him and locked an arm behind his back. He wrapped his other arm around his necking, pulling his head back with a strong choke hold. He held it for a good minute until the intruder passed out.

Maurice's heart was pounding, as if he had just escaped a tiger's grip. He felt a warm stream running down his face. He didn't realize how badly he was hurt until he saw all the blood starting to soak into his yellow T-shirt. His arms stung from cuts from the broken glass that was on the floor.

Partially blinded by the blood running down his face, he wiped off some of the blood with his T-shirt. Julian was still on the floor but was trying to sit up. He was badly beaten with cuts on his face and arms. He was holding his left hand, which was bleeding profusely, and his shirt was all but torn off.

Maurice crawled over to Julian. He tore off a strip of what was left of Julian's bloody shirt and wrapped it around Julian's forearm tightly to slow down the bleeding. Tearing off another piece, he wrapped it around the deep gouge in his hand.

Julian struggled to yell, "Maurice, behind you!"

Maurice turned around, and everything went dark.

When Maurice came to minutes later, he was on the floor with his head cradled in Julian's arms.

"He almost got us, man. He almost got us." Julian's free arm was bloodied but not badly cut. He had it wrapped around Maurice's chest.

Maurice was dazed but started to come to his senses. He groaned and tried to sit up, but Julian held him tightly. "Stay still for a minute," insisted Julian. "I don't know how badly you're hurt."

There was a large pool of blood in the middle of the kitchen. It was hard to tell who it came from, but more than likely all three men made a contribution.

After a few moments, Maurice pushed himself away from Julian's loose grip. Maurice could see that they both were weak from all the blood they had lost.

"Damn." Maurice groaned again. He clutched his stomach, which had a gash across just above his navel. He glanced at his arms and legs; they looked okay. There was still a trickle of blood running down his face, but Julian had managed to wrap a small piece of clothing around his head, covering a cut above his left eye.

"Where is he?" asked Maurice. "I thought I had knocked him out."

Julian answered in slurred speech, "I thought so too, but he got up and gave you a wallop on the head. He stumbled down the hall. I think he was badly hurt and panicked."

"You look terrible, Julian. Do you think you can stand up?" Maurice started to move but grimaced again in pain and stopped.

Julian nodded. "I'm so sorry you had to be part of this, Maurice. By the way, you look pretty awful yourself." Maurice's red curls were splattered with darker blotches of blood.

Maurice shook his head and managed a weak smile upon realizing they had survived this round. He imagined how terrible they both must have looked. Julian let out a halfhearted laugh.

"When I first heard the commotion, I thought I was having a bad dream." Maurice groaned as he held his hand against his stomach. "I didn't recognize the language you were both speaking. I assume this guy was from the same group that's been after you, right?"

"Yes, he was," replied Julian. "We were speaking Moroccan Arabic."

They were still sitting on the floor side by side, each leaning against the kitchen cabinets.

"Julian, here ... hold onto this cabinet handle. I'm gonna try to get up and get you on a chair." Maurice placed Julian's good arm against the cabinet and rested his hand by the handle. "You got it?" he asked Julian.

"Yeah, thanks." Julian held loosely onto the cabinet.

Maurice rolled on his side and gave a holler as he lifted himself to his knees. Using the chair next to him, he managed to pull himself up to a standing position. Still wobbly, he took a deep breath and held onto the countertop. He leaned over Julian, extended one arm, and started to lift him to his knees.

At that moment Euphrates walked in. He stood frozen in the doorway, shaking his head in disbelief. Then he screamed something unintelligible. He put his hands first to his head and then swung his arms out in front of him. He was signing so rapidly that he seemed to be rearranging the air in front of him.

Julian made a feeble attempt to sign something to Euphrates, but all he could do was nod.

Euphrates lifted Julian up off of his knees. Julian yelled in pain, but Euphrates carried him to one of the comfortable lounges on the patio. He propped up Julian's bad arm and hand on a pillow.

Maurice, who had been leaning against the kitchen counter, suddenly fell to the floor. He had passed out.

When Maurice came to, he was lying on a lounge chair next to

Julian. He looked up at Euphrates, who motioned to him to remain still.

Euphrates lay down next to Julian and cradled his head on his chest. Euphrates's shirt and pants were now bloodstained, as well.

Maurice watched Julian struggle to sign something to Euphrates. He heard him mumble, "Maurice saved me." Julian then laid his head back on Euphrates's chest and closed his eyes.

Maurice watched Euphrates gently stroke Julian's head as he held him in an embrace. He began to cry.

There was a silence at Asilomar as never before.

Over the next week there were good days and bad days. Euphrates had run down the hill to get Fina the day of the struggle. She called a local doctor to treat both Julian and Maurice. While their wounds looked frightening, they were not life threatening. The doctor wanted them both to go to the hospital to be thoroughly checked out, but they resisted. The doctor did his best to stitch them up. Julian's wrist was sprained and required a splint and arm sling. The doctor left them a bottle of painkillers that Fina administered against their protests.

Fina temporarily closed her bakery and moved into Asilomar to help Euphrates take care of the battle-weary fighters. Of course, she brought baby Julian, who was a positive distraction and source of joy and amusement for them.

After the first altercation a couple of weeks earlier, Julian told Maurice that he was going to suspend plans for guests for the indefinite future—Claire being the only exception, of course. He said the current threats he faced made Asilomar anything but a peaceful refuge.

He also said that Euphrates decided to close down his booth permanently. Julian told Maurice that with three men in the house, the intruders might think twice before approaching again. Julian did relent and agreed to have locks installed on the front and rear doors.

Maurice recovered quickly from his physical wounds, but he was afraid there would always be a scar across his stomach. After replaying the fight in his mind, he was grateful he had remembered some of his college wrestling moves.

But it wasn't the physical wounds that troubled him most. He was emotionally traumatized by the entire ordeal and withdrew to his casita for the first couple of days. Euphrates made several attempts to talk with him, but Maurice put him off, needing time to sort out the confusing emotions that made him want to isolate himself from everyone.

Maurice needed time to be alone and would often walk to the old windmill down the road. He'd sit there for hours, looking up and imagining how ages ago, the now naked blades would be dressed in billowing cloth sails, inviting the wind to breathe life into the giant windmill—the same windmills that Don Quixote mistook for enemy soldiers. Maurice questioned if his decision to stay there was a mistake, if he was imagining something that wasn't there. Was he also pursuing an illusion that was disguised as a dream?

While he had grown to trust Julian, he was beginning to doubt if it was all worth it. Since the fight, Euphrates's attitude toward Maurice had changed. Even though he demonstrated a greater interest in Maurice's well-being, Maurice questioned whether it would be healthy for him to pursue any mutual attraction that existed. His past experiences with troubled and sometimes violent relationships made him retreat from interaction with everyone. He even considered ending his vacation and returning home.

One morning Euphrates left a note on Maurice's front door. It read, "Dear Maurice. We are worried about you, especially me. Like Julian, I still feel you were meant to be here. We are all here for you."

The note was a turning point for Maurice. Those simple words "meant to be here" had become an irresistible mantra since arriving at Asilomar, and he believed Euphrates's sentiments were genuine. He showered, got dressed, and walked briskly to the patio, where Fina and Euphrates were having breakfast.

Euphrates stood up and gave Maurice a hug and, to his welcome surprise, a kiss on each cheek.

Fina said, "Maurice, I'm so glad you're back with us. You're family, and we need you."

Maurice smiled and replied, "I'm sorry. I guess I just needed time to process everything that's happened in the past couple of weeks. I missed you guys too."

He sat down and turned toward Euphrates and mouthed, "Thank you."

Julian's wounds were more serious, as they had compounded the ones he had received in the previous altercation. He spent the first week in bed. During that time Maurice could hear the same music coming from his room each morning during breakfast. It was the second movement of Rodrigo's *El Concierto de Aranjuez*. Unlike the first and third movements, the second was led by a slow yet intense classical guitar. Because of its wistful resonance Maurice referred to it as *Julian's lament*.

During the following week, Euphrates divided his time between Julian and Maurice. Fina explained to Maurice that Julian was like the brother he never had and that Maurice had become somewhat of a hero in Euphrates's eyes. After Julian recovered enough to leave the confines of his bedroom, the three of them became inseparable. They spent hours together, talking, enjoying the security of one another's company, and playing with little Julian. Maurice had started to call him little J for short.

Still, Julian would spend a good part of his time sleeping. Neither Euphrates nor Maurice wanted to leave his side. Euphrates would read, and Maurice kept busy typing notes on his laptop.

One day Maurice wrote a note to Euphrates: "Do you have a textbook about sign language that I could study?" Maurice noticed a big smile come across Euphrates's face when he read the note. He immediately ran up to his room and returned with an old sign language textbook. After that, Maurice spent hours studying and practicing signing, often at the amusement of Euphrates.

One morning, Maurice was sitting on the patio lounge chair, paging through the signing textbook. He was looking at the illustrations and trying to mimic what he saw with his own gestures. Euphrates walked over and surprised Maurice and sat next to him on the lounge chair.

He put his right arm around Maurice and signed something with his left hand.

"Good morning, Euphrates." Maurice replied in sign as he felt Euphrates's leg pressed against his. Once again Maurice noticed a hint of incense, but this time he was overwhelmed by a manly scent, and it was most pleasant. It was reminiscent of the first day they met but seemed more intense as Euphrates leaned against him.

He tapped Maurice's shoulder to get his attention and turned to face him. His large brown eyes and broad lips were within inches of his face. Maurice suddenly realized that his hand was resting on Euphrates's thigh. He pulled it back suddenly after feeling self-conscious.

Euphrates turned to a page in the book and pointed to a sign that was illustrated on top of the page. He mumbled softly as he pointed. "Thank you."

Euphrates and Maurice had never shared any physical contact before. Maurice felt an excitement run through his body. He was glad that Euphrates felt comfortable to approach him, but it was more than that. Maurice had always found him attractive, and the sexual energy that morning was evident. Feeling Euphrates's long arm wrap around him created a nervous knot in his stomach. It was a sensation that he hadn't felt in years.

Maurice responded to Euphrates's approach by squeezing tighter on his leg. He quickly paged through the sign book for an appropriate sign to point to. He found one, the equivalent of "We are friends."

Without hesitation, Euphrates gave Maurice a gentle kiss on each cheek and got up to go to the kitchen.

It was clear that Euphrates's attitude toward Maurice had been greatly altered by the fight. While he initially felt he was viewed with some suspicion as an uninvited stranger, Maurice now felt that he had earned Euphrates's respect.

Maurice was finally beginning to feel like maybe he was meant to be there.

As soon as he felt good enough to cook, Maurice took a lead in the kitchen. Fina had her hands full taking care of the two Julians. While his dinners were basic, everyone seemed satisfied. Julian, Fina, and baby Julian would take their places at the table. Euphrates would bring out the wine and bread, as he always had done, and Maurice would bring out the dinner.

One evening Maurice came to the other side of the table to hold a large platter of fried fish while Fina served herself. As he walked around to the other side where Julian was sitting, he passed Euphrates, who hadn't yet taken his seat. As he passed, Euphrates affectionately ran his hand down Maurice's back.

As Maurice leaned over to serve Julian, who was constrained by his sling, Julian whispered, "I'm glad you and Euphrates are becoming close. I was hoping that would happen."

Maurice blushed and gave Julian a little wink.

Maurice had cooked merluza, a local fish that Fina had brought from town. Imitating what he had seen in some of the local restaurants, he sliced the whole fish in half lengthwise, head and tail intact. The halves were fried until golden brown and complemented by a generous helping of fried potatoes and a small salad of lettuce and tomato—a simple but an impressive effort.

As they started to enjoy the fish, Euphrates waved his hands, pointing to Maurice. He signed, "Delicious."

Julian said, "Maurice, you know Euphrates had rarely tried to speak with anyone but me. You can't imagine what that means to me." The moisture welling up in Julian's eyes brought silence to the table.

Maurice looked at Euphrates. They stared at one another for a few moments. Maurice again felt that nervous knot in his stomach. He smiled and signed the first sign that Euphrates had shown him in the book, "Thank you."

Julian added, "You know, Maurice, I'm forever indebted to you. I will never forget what you did."

Maurice didn't know what to say. He reached over and touched Julian's hand and gave it a light squeeze.

A few more days passed. Maurice was feeling much more like himself, and Julian's spirits were improving as well.

One morning while Maurice was having toast and coffee with Fina and Euphrates, Julian walked out to the patio with a book cradled in his arm. He sat next to Maurice.

"Maurice, with all that's gone on lately, I haven't really asked you how you're doing. I don't mean recovering from the fight but rather with regard to the original reason you're here, your search for 'freedom and courage,' as you put it." As usual, Julian maintained full eye contact with Maurice as he spoke.

Maurice replied, "I've been writing a lot of notes lately, but I still haven't thought of a way to tie it all together. I feel more confident that there's a story inside me. Just not sure yet how to make it come alive."

Julian took the book that he had in his arm and laid it on the table in front of him. It was the guestbook.

Euphrates's and Fina's eyes were fixed on the book, as if certain powers were hidden within its gold-trimmed pages.

"I feel I have a different relationship with you than with other guests that have passed through Asilomar. I generally keep other guests' entries confidential, but as a friend, not a guest, I thought I'd share some of the experiences we've had with previous visitors. We talked about Claire's experience, and I think you might benefit from hearing some of the other stories. Maybe it will inspire the story that's inside of you."

Euphrates knocked gently on the table. When Maurice looked back, Euphrates smiled and made an "okay" sign with his hands.

"Yes, of course, that would be wonderful. I'm honored that you would even consider that, Julian."

"Well, how about we start with one entry in the book from a couple of years ago. Fina, would you mind bringing us some more coffee and churros? I'd ask Euphrates but if I tried to sign with one hand, I'm not sure what would come out." He giggled for the first time since the fight.

Fina replied to Julian as she stroked his shoulder, "Of course, *mi amor.*" She caught herself and rushed off to the kitchen.

It was the first time Maurice had witnessed such an obvious display of affection between Fina and Julian. Maurice looked at Euphrates, who returned his glance with a wink and a subtle nod.

Fina came back with more coffee and some warm churros. Sucre followed her to the kitchen. She was rarely denied a treat.

As Fina filled Julian's cup with coffee, Julian whispered something to her. She smiled and gave his head a couple of gentle strokes.

Again, the loving exchange didn't go unnoticed by Maurice. It was clear that Julian and Fina felt they no longer had reason to hide their affection for one another.

Julian motioned for Euphrates to come sit beside him.

Julian opened the ornately bound book. He had already placed several sticky notes of different colors on various pages. He opened it to the green marker and ran his finger down the page.

"Oh, yes, Devin," Julian proudly announced.

Euphrates nodded his approval.

Julian continued, "Devin was a young man who worked in the galley of a cruise ship. Although he was a cook, he did have previous training as a chef in a culinary school in the United States. As a matter of fact, I think Claire had met him on a cruise and was responsible for him visiting us."

"Well, Devin's ship had stopped for a maintenance check for a number of days in Almería, just south of here. When he asked if he could visit, it turned out that the timing was perfect, as we had only two other guests. He arrived one morning and signed in with this message: 'To be the chef of my own restaurant.'"

Maurice commented, "Sounds simple enough."

"Well," continued Julian, "things aren't always as simple as they might seem."

"I guess I should know that," Maurice added with a modest shrug of embarrassment.

"It turned out that Devin had a partner at home. Tom was an attorney. While Devin said that Tom claimed to love him, he was very controlling and apparently he wasn't supportive of Devin's dream of being a chef, let alone of having his own restaurant. According to Devin, he was always finding negative reasons why it was just a silly pipe dream. 'Very risky,' 'No money in it,' 'We wouldn't have any time to spend together,' 'I might want to relocate to the East Coast to a larger law firm,' and the worst one, 'Are you sure you're a good enough chef to have your own restaurant?' Does this ring a bell with something we discussed not long ago, Maurice?"

Maurice thought for a moment and then replied, "Yes, that

quote in the hallway, about sharing your secret with someone and your destiny may be altered."

"Yes," said Julian, smiling like a happy professor whose prize student had come up with the correct answer, "except in this case, Devin shared it with someone who was not supportive. Tom was more interested in his own dream and discounted what was important to Devin."

Julian continued, "Devin asked me, 'Why is this so hard? I feel guilty and angry.' I told him that we all find ourselves between rocks and hard places at times. I explained that he was feeling guilty about putting his goals before those of his friend, and that he was angry because he was *here* and wanted to be *there*, meaning he was supporting Tom's needs and desires, but what he really wanted and needed was to be out there pursuing his own dream."

Maurice asked, "So how did Devin resolve this, or didn't he?"

"Well, first, I helped Devin peel back the layers of fear and doubt that were holding him back. He lacked two things: self-confidence and opportunity. He also suffered in a relationship that wasn't healthy. I could help him with the first two, but with regard to the relationship I told him he had to make that major decision on his own."

Julian paused and sipped some coffee. He reached across the table to grab one of the churros.

Maurice remembered he had his notepad in his back pocket. He pulled it out and asked, "Julian, would you mind if I jotted down some notes?"

Julian shook his head. "No, not at all."

Fina heard little Julian crying and went inside to check on him.

Julian commented, "Not to change the subject, but that little guy is one of the reasons I'm so happy that we are becoming a family. I need both Euphrates's and your support." He was looking at Maurice when he spoke.

Maurice didn't reply but was flattered by Julian's support and friendship. Still, he wasn't quite sure what he meant by family.

Julian continued with Devin's adventure. "Devin stayed with us for four nights. I asked him if he would create a menu for each night and prepare a meal for us and the rest of the guests, about five people in total. I told him that Euphrates and I would be his assistants in the kitchen and would accept any assignment he would give us."

Julian paused for another sip of coffee. "Well, Devin was mortified at first. Then I told him that since we didn't have any obligation to provide guests dinner, he could prepare dinner the first night just for us. He'd be able to get used to the kitchen and work through his nerves. Fina even volunteered to help him shop for supplies in town. He agreed. That first night we ate inside to make it more of a private affair."

Julian wrote on a piece of paper and gave it to Euphrates. Julian had written, "Pacha, how did that first night turn out?"

Euphrates smiled and gave him a thumbs-up.

Julian said, "It was a great dinner, and with that success behind him, I suggested to Devin that he cook for all the guests the next night. I told him that I was sure he would delight them with his cooking.

"The next two nights he cooked for everyone, and they all were great successes. But for the third and final night there was one additional attendee that I invited. Ricardo Castello wasn't a guest at Asilomar but instead was an old friend and executive chef of one of the finest restaurants in Granada. We had become well acquainted when I was at the university. He catered for several of our symposiums.

"Anyway, by the final night, Devin's nerves had calmed and he was beginning to get more daring and creative. He prepared a four-course dinner. Euphrates and I acted as servers. The guests quietly ate their dinner, complimenting Devin as they had the previous nights. Devin noticed the new guest but didn't think anything of it at the time.

"Afterwards, Euphrates and I served the dessert, a cheesecake with fig sauce. Yum! I still remember it. A tiny glass of dessert wine was served, and dinner was over. The guests went their separate ways … all but one.

"Devin was busy in the kitchen cleaning up. l called him to come out for a moment and enjoy a coffee with us. He started to go back to the kitchen to get cups and the coffee, but I told him to sit down. Euphrates would get it."

Maurice was leaning over the table and listening so intently that he almost knocked over his coffee cup, which was still full. The sweetness of Fina's churros, which he loved, caught his attention and he took one and dipped it in his coffee.

"I asked Devin to sit down and introduced him to Ricardo. Ricardo complimented him on the dinner. Still, Devin had no idea who he was.

"The chef asked, 'Devin, I understand that cooking is your passion, is that correct?' When Devin agreed that it was, Chef Ricardo replied, 'That's an ambitious dream to have. It takes a lot of hard work, and the restaurant business is more complicated than most people realize. There is a lot to learn, but if you have the desire and the heart for it, the rewards can be endless.' Devin listened politely, but you could tell he was wondering who this man was.

"Chef Ricardo finally introduced himself. 'Devin, I am the executive chef of El Rincón Criollo in Granada. You may have heard of us. We are one of the few five-star restaurants in all of Andalucia.' Devin's jaw dropped. 'How would you like to come to work at my restaurant as Chef Tournant? I have an opening right now that I need to fill right away, and I'm very impressed with your cooking skills. It's a demanding position, but it's an opportunity for you to sharpen your culinary skills and learn the restaurant business. Who knows where it could lead? What do you say?'"

Maurice said, "I imagine he was almost speechless at this point."

"Yes, he was. The chef told him to think about it and to let him know in a couple of days, as he wanted to fill this position as soon as possible. Devin thanked the chef and said he would give it serious thought.

"Devin and I were up a good part of the night talking after the chef left. He shared a list of his concerns about making such a huge decision. As we went through each concern, he realized they were just excuses, except for one—his partner. Devin said, 'I think I should ask Tom if it's okay to do this, but I'm afraid he'll get mad.'

"I asked Devin, 'Do you think Tom would ask for your permission to move to the East Coast to join another law firm?' He shook his head to say no."

Fina returned from the house and brought some fresh coffee and more churros to the table. Julian refilled his cup before continuing.

"I asked him if he cared deeply for someone whose creative spirit or career ambition called them to another place, would he try to convince them to stay, or would he set them free to follow that dream?"

Julian imitated Devin, flapping his hands upward like a bird in flight.

"I told him I couldn't make that decision for him, but I did say that part of loving someone means supporting that person, and that while Tom may indeed love him, his unwillingness to support Devin may indicate that he loves himself more. Devin confessed that he feared losing his friend forever."

Maurice took a bite of his churro and shook his head. "That's a tough position to be in."

Julian said he advised him that some people who are too fearful to risk pursuing their own dream may often place obstacles in front of others to discourage their own quest.

Julian explained that Devin's defense was that his friend Tom promised that if he moved to a new job on the East Coast, he could look for a chef's job then.

"I just shook my head. 'Devin, that sounds like old poison in a new bottle. An old friend once told me, "Don't let people live rent free in your head." Follow your heart.'

"Devin was painfully conflicted that night. I noticed him sitting alone on the patio for hours. When I saw him the next morning, he looked scared and nervous, but he was smiling. He said, 'Julian, I prayed last night for an answer. I'm going to take the job. I called Tom, and he yelled at me last night, saying things that I never knew he was capable of, calling me selfish and insensitive. It contrasted so with the love and support I've received here in just the past few days. My decision was easier than I had expected.'"

At the conclusion, Euphrates outstretched his arms in celebration.

Maurice commented, "You must feel gratified to see stories end this way. Perhaps Devin's faith helped him make the final decision. I'm sure they are not all success stories but—"

Julian interrupted, "Perhaps his personal faith did help him to make that decision, but one thing I avoid is discussing religion." Julian sipped his coffee. "My personal beliefs are irrelevant to others, but if you want to know, I believe in the power of the universe. Kismet, karma, fate—they are not to be confused with coincidence. What's most important is how we recognize the destiny that the universe bestows on us, how we interact and take advantage of the opportunities it gives us, and how we accept the demands it makes upon us. Control is an illusion, but we have power in recognizing when doors are open, seizing the moment to walk through the opening, being willing to risk comfort and security for the chance to experience exhilaration and self-realization."

Julian gently squeezed Maurice's arm. "Maurice, part of my dream is to be able to help others to reach theirs. You know, sometimes the universe conspires to work with us. You just need to be able to recognize when that's happening. In Devin's case, it didn't hurt to give the old universe a little nudge. I was glad to be able to provide that open door to Devin and give him a little push."

Euphrates tapped on the table to get Julian's attention and signed something to him. Julian acknowledged, saying, "Euphrates wants me to read to you what I first entered into the guestbook. Hee hee, it's the very first entry."

He turned the guestbook back to the very first page and read, "'Julian. June 17, 2006. To enable the confused and the fearful in pursuit of their passions and dreams.'" Julian confessed, "Guess that sounds pretty grandiose, but I always have been sincere in wanting to help people. I loved teaching at the university, but after a course would end I wasn't always sure what impact I really had on anyone. I wanted to feel like I was making a difference in someone's life, and I think Asilomar has been my vehicle for that. My personal life in terms of relationships has not been as fulfilling, but I can deal with that. Perhaps that's one reason why I put so much energy into Asilomar. I accept where I am today, and I'm happy. Now my only dream is for my son, little Julian, to have all the opportunities possible. I want and need nothing more than that."

Maurice was struck by Julian's selflessness and generosity. He couldn't help but notice that his eyes welled up with pride as he spoke of Devin's breakthrough.

"Well, that was more exhausting than I thought it would be," joked Julian. "Time for a nap."

Fina added, "I'll clean up the kitchen. You boys go out and enjoy the day."

Maurice said, "Fina, why don't Euphrates and I take little J out in the garden for a while. It will give you a break and let us have some fun with him."

Fina sighed. "Ah, that would be great! Thanks."

Maurice noticed Fina and Julian exchanging affectionate glances. He figured they were eager to seize an opportunity to share some private time together.

Euphrates went inside to get little J, who was already dressed in a little denim outfit with suspenders and a long-sleeved T-shirt. He carried him out to the garden. Sucre ran circles around all three of them. Little Julian would mumble "Oof, oof" for Euphrates's name. He hadn't quite yet learned how to address Maurice.

Euphrates rolled around in the grass with little Julian. They were both laughing. Maurice sprawled out in the sun a few feet away. No sooner was he on the ground than the youngster ran to him and jumped on his chest.

"Ouch," mocked Maurice, pretending it hurt. The youngster ran back and forth between the two until he tired.

After a while, Euphrates picked up little Julian and held him up on his shoulder. He signaled to Maurice to follow him. As they walked, Euphrates pointed to Maurice, then pointed to little Julian, and then gestured back to Maurice.

Maurice assumed that Euphrates was asking if he liked children, as well, and in particular, little Julian. Maurice wrote a short note on the pad of paper: "Yes, I always wished I could have had children."

Euphrates nodded with an approving smile.

Maurice followed Euphrates to the "secret garden," as Maurice liked to refer to it. They entered through the iron gate.

Euphrates set little Julian down and let him run around the fountain. He was fascinated with the gurgling water.

Maurice could feel the grip of Euphrates's large hand wrap around his arm as he walked him a full revolution around the fountain. Maurice recalled his first day when he and Claire were talking about the initials in the tiles. Before she had the chance to explain their significance, Euphrates had interrupted and led them back to the house for dinner.

Euphrates led him to the location of one of the tiles that was placed by the "SE," or southeast directional. The initials spelled "JTB." He pointed to them and then pointed and waved toward the house.

He kept waving his finger at the house until Maurice said, "Julian?"

Euphrates affirmed that they were Julian's initials in the tile. He wrote on a piece of paper, "Julian Tarik Bakkar." He then pointed to the southeast. He waved his arm toward the ocean, as if saying, "Farther, farther that way."

Maurice didn't quite understand what he was trying to say. Euphrates again pointed to the tile and then out toward the ocean.

Euphrates reached over, took the notepad out of Maurice's pocket, and scribbled, "Morocco."

Maurice nodded and said, "Oh, yes, Julian is from Morocco."

Euphrates then walked Maurice around the fountain between the north and west markers to the tile that had the initials "EB." Again, Euphrates pointed down to the tile, then to his chest, and then to the northwest over the mountains behind them.

Maurice responded, "Your initials"—he pointed to northern Spain—"that's where you're from."

Euphrates displayed a big smile and wrote on the notepad, "Euphrates Baroja. Bilbao, Spain." He put his arm around Maurice, giving him a gentle hug.

Euphrates took a moment to jot something else on the pad and handed it to Maurice. It said, "I built fountain and garden for Julian. Best friend ever."

Touched, Maurice took the notepad and wrote, "You are rich in friendship." He handed the note to Euphrates.

He took Maurice's hand and placed it over his heart. Euphrates looked into Maurice's eyes and wrote a short note. "Us too."

To Maurice's surprise Euphrates pulled him to his chest and held him in a long embrace. The warmth of Euphrates's body against him felt comforting. The tightness of his arms around him was sending another message that they both understood but had never admitted to one another. Maurice did not want to make eye contact, as he could feel his hormones stirring. From their close embrace, he sensed that Euphrates felt the same. The tender moment was interrupted by a tug on Euphrates's tunic.

It was little Julian. He was starting to get tired. Euphrates scooped him up off the ground where he had been sitting, and they walked back to the house. Fina took over little Julian duties while Euphrates and Maurice went out on the patio. Euphrates wrote something on the pad and gave it to Maurice.

"Let me take you down the cliff to our beach, okay?"

Maurice nodded and said, "Yes, let's go!"

Euphrates held up his hand to say, "Wait one minute." He went into the kitchen and was gone for about five minutes.

He returned with a small knapsack. He opened it up to show Maurice. Inside was a bottle of wine, bread, and some smoked sausage. Euphrates led him to the edge of the patio and signaled to Maurice to follow.

Love's Discovery

Euphrates's long legs easily negotiated the four-foot stucco wall at the edge of the patio. Maurice paused and looked out over the cliff at the ocean and then down at the steep embankment. He used one hand to balance himself on the wall while he lifted his short legs over one at a time.

Euphrates looked at him and laughed. He put one of his hands out to his waist, making fun of Maurice's height. Maurice shot back by rolling back the sleeve of his T-shirt and flexing his bicep.

For the first time since he left home, Maurice felt a level of comfort that surprised him. It had been just two weeks since he arrived, yet in spite of the attack on him and Julian, he felt secure, relaxed, and wanted.

It was a steep and winding climb down the cliff. The path was a crude trail of steep switchbacks. As he descended, Maurice was tempted to look up at the spectacular view, but Euphrates would look back and yell to get his attention, instructing him to keep his eye on the path. After ten minutes of slow descent, they reached the bottom.

Maurice stopped and panned from one end of the crescent beach to the other. It wasn't more than several hundred yards long and about fifty yards deep. On either end of the beach, rocky cliffs stretched out to meet the ocean, sealing off any access to the beach except from the water or the path they had just descended.

He bent down and picked up a handful of sand. "This is like sugar," he commented as he watched Euphrates read his lips. He pretended to sprinkle some in his mouth.

The surf was strong enough to create a mist as the waves broke close to the beach. Occasionally, they would make a thud as a large breaker would crash against the shallow ocean floor.

Euphrates put his arm around Maurice's waist. Maurice reciprocated and pulled him as tight to his body as he could. It was his way of communicating how nice he was feeling and how nice Euphrates felt to him.

Euphrates's body was slender but firm, and even among the salt air Maurice could detect Euphrates's sweet yet musky smell. It excited Maurice, but he made a conscious effort to try to focus on other scenery.

Euphrates walked them halfway down the beach to a little cove that had a huge rock formation reaching out over the beach.

He let go of Maurice and spread out a small blanket he had in the knapsack. After carefully arranging the wine and food on the edge of the blanket, Euphrates leaned back on his elbows facing the water. His T-shirt had pulled up above his pants, exposing a line of black curly hair that came from below his navel up his stomach and disappeared under the T-shirt.

It was too much for Maurice, who had been suppressing his feelings for days. Hoping he wouldn't offend Euphrates by being too aggressive, he moved close to him and put his large hand on Euphrates's stomach. His fingers followed the line of short curly hair protruding from above his belt up to his T-shirt. Euphrates didn't move or turn his head.

While Maurice worried that maybe he was being too forward, Euphrates caught him off guard and rolled over on top of Maurice and started to kiss him, first on the forehead and then on the ears and cheeks. His put his wet lips to Maurice's chin and moved them slowly to his mouth. Maurice quietly groaned with pleasure.

Maurice thought to himself, *His kisses are like sunlight on my face.* Euphrates pulled away a few inches from Maurice's face to look at him. He stared at Maurice with those large dark-brown sunken eyes. Maurice would never forget that first taste of Euphrates.

For an hour they played, explored, kissed, laughed, touched, tasted, and smelled. They began to know each other in almost every way they could.

After a while, Euphrates sat up and instructed Maurice to sit in front of him, facing the ocean. Euphrates wrapped his arms around him and nuzzled his head against his red curls that were covered with salty ocean mist. He whispered in Maurice's ear, "Maybe meant to be too."

Maurice was astounded by how clearly he uttered those words. It was as if he had been rehearsing them. Maurice turned and looked up. Euphrates was quietly sobbing. Maurice could tell that all the emotion of what had happened to Julian, the imminent threats that still hung over Asilomar, and the unexpected arrival of Maurice had accumulated and overwhelmed him.

After their moments of intimacy passed, Maurice opened the bottle of wine while Euphrates sliced the bread and sausage. They spent the next hour silently enjoying one another's company. They exchanged a few written notes. Maurice read one note from Euphrates that made him well up all over again. It read, "The universe answered my dream for someone in my life." He then held up the note that Maurice had given him the day before. It was crinkled up, but Euphrates held it up with such pride. It originally read, "Rich in friendship." Euphrates altered it to say, "Rich in ~~friendship~~ love."

Maurice signed yes and smothered Euphrates with a round of kisses that led from the back of his neck around to his chin and back to Euphrates's sexy lips.

They didn't do anything serious that afternoon but be playful and affectionate. It was all that was needed for Maurice to know that something special was happening.

After they finished off the wine, they slowly made their way back up the cliff. When they reached the patio, they both were panting from the climb. Fina brought out a big pitcher of lemonade.

"Thanks, Fina. This looks so good!" exclaimed Maurice, who was thirsty from the wine and cheese, the salt air, and of course, the kissing.

"Did you boys enjoy the beach?" she asked.

Euphrates gave Fina a hug and then pointed to Maurice. He gestured to say that they were special friends. Fina nodded.

She continued, "Julian has been resting all afternoon. I know when he gets up he'll be hungry. Do you boys mind eating a bit earlier tonight?"

Because of the excitement over their first romantic connection, the wine and bread they ate on the beach had done nothing to diminish their appetites. They both nodded yes.

Fina replied, "Okay, probably in an hour or so. I'll ring the bell when we're ready."

Euphrates signaled for Maurice to follow him as he went down the hallway that led to the front reception area. He walked up the stairs that Maurice had noticed on his first day. At the top was a small arched doorway. As soon as Euphrates opened the door, a gust of the ocean air rushed by them.

Maurice followed Euphrates into a small but cozy room. The scent of incense that greeted him came as no surprise. The room was an odd shape, almost triangular but with a little round area in the far corner where there was a large open window that faced out to the sea. The breeze was banging the wooden shutter against the wall, so Euphrates closed it. In the round corner was a chair and small desk with several books. A double bed was against one wall and a small dresser on the other. There was a small door that led to a bathroom, which had a colorfully tiled shower and a little porthole-shaped window also overlooking the sea.

Euphrates opened his arms wide, signaling, "This is where I live."

Maurice noticed that hanging over his bedroom door there was a silver hamsa about six inches tall. It was intricate in its detail with an amber gemstone mounted in the palm of the hand.

Maurice pointed to it and signed, "I love it."

Euphrates walked to the desk and opened the top drawer. He removed a little box and brought it over to Maurice. After opening the lid, he carefully removed a small silver hamsa charm. It was much like the one he wore. He put it in Maurice's open palm and squeezed his hand shut.

He pointed to his heart and then to Maurice's and smiled.

Maurice gave him a big hug. Since Maurice was at least eight or nine inches shorter than Euphrates, he reached no farther than Euphrates's chest, but it felt wonderful.

With his signing knowledge still limited, Maurice wrote on the notepad that he wanted to go to the casita and get cleaned up before dinner. Euphrates signaled his agreement. Maurice headed downstairs and down the hall to the patio. Julian was sitting in a lounge chair and caught Maurice's attention before he could say anything.

"Maurice," commented Julian, "I understand Euphrates took you down to the beach."

"Julian, it was wonderful, and so private. We brought some wine and got to know one another better." He thought that was a tactful way of putting it.

"I hope you did. You mean a lot to both Euphrates and me, and I know that he feels very strongly for you." Julian paused and glanced to see if Euphrates was nearby. He continued, "I hope you develop a serious relationship with one another, for a number of reasons. Of course, I think you guys would make a great couple, and for selfish reasons, I would like to feel that I have a family."

Julian's eyes became moist as he slid his hand over his lips. "I can't totally understand something that I never really had, but what I see developing between both of you makes me very happy."

Maurice was surprised to see Julian get so personal, but then again, little would surprise him anymore at Asilomar. He was relieved that Julian felt supportive of whatever was happening between him and Euphrates. He wasn't sure quite what it was himself, but he knew it felt good.

On his way back to his casita, Maurice thought, *Man, is every day at Asilomar so extraordinary? Or is extraordinary the ordinary here?*

Left with that thought, he took a long shower and got dressed for dinner.

Maurice was already out the door as the dinner chime sounded. It was a typical evening—the sun was low in the sky, the moisture from the ocean crept inland, and a new population of scents from the garden drifted across the patio.

Euphrates was out on the patio playing with little Julian. Sucre ran up to Maurice as soon as she saw him walking up the pathway.

"Hey, girl, how you doing?"

He ran around in a circle a couple of times with Sucre chasing him. The old girl moved slowly, and it was easy for him to outrun her, but she still had a little puppy left inside of her.

"Okay, you two, time to eat!" Fina yelled.

Maurice arrived at the dinner table, where Euphrates and Julian were already seated. He was about to take his usual seat across from Euphrates when Julian pointed to the empty chair next to Euphrates.

Maurice walked around the table and took his seat. Euphrates put his hand on Maurice's leg and gave it a soft squeeze.

Fina had baked sea bass with asparagus and Spanish rice. The aroma from the steaming dish filled the patio. Julian tapped on the table to get everyone's attention.

Maurice noticed that Euphrates was staring at him and raised his hands to his shoulders in a questioning gesture.

Euphrates signed something to Julian, and Julian explained, "Euphrates is amused by your red curls standing on end."

Maurice tapped the top of his head with his hand, and everyone laughed.

"Maurice, would you like to give the toast tonight?" Julian asked. His raised eyebrows indicated that it was more of a request than an invitation.

"Yes, I'd love to." Maurice raised his wineglass and repeated the toast they had said for the past two weeks. "May your journeys be long and your dreams be forever. *Salud*."

"I really had a good rest today," commented Julian. "I feel so much better than I have lately. The bandage just came off, and as you can see I'm operating in full arm mode. No sling!" He held up both arms proudly. His signing to Euphrates was still a bit clumsy due to his hand having been bandaged for so long.

"That means we can put him to work now," joked Fina.

Little Julian was sitting in a high chair next to his father. He was making gurgling noises and was dropping bits of food below to an accommodating Sucre.

During dinner, Maurice was busy telling Fina about their hike to the beach, omitting certain parts of the story he deemed inappropriate.

At one point Maurice saw Euphrates waving his hand, trying to get Julian's attention. Maurice noticed that Julian did seem distracted. Euphrates finally tapped on the table to get Julian's attention.

Julian acknowledged Euphrates and said, "Excuse me, there's something I want to tell everyone."

Fina and Maurice immediately turned their attention toward Julian.

Julian rubbed his hand across the back of little Julian's head. "This little fellow is the reason I live now. His well-being is all that matters to me."

He gave a glance around the table and continued, signing slowly as he spoke. "This is important."

Maurice wondered what it could be that suddenly brought Julian to such a serious moment.

Julian continued but signed slowly because of his bandaged hand. "Last week I had an attorney come by and draw up some legal documents that concern little Julian. I know that there is a strong possibility I may not live to see him grow to manhood. I want him to be a good man, a strong man. He needs to know he's loved unconditionally and given every opportunity that I have had and more."

Upon hearing him say he may not be around to see little Julian grow up, Fina let out an audible sigh of protest.

With his eyes becoming watery, Julian explained, "I am asking Euphrates to be little Julian's guardian. If anything would happen to me, then I'd like you, Pacha, to be responsible for him. I know this is a heavy responsibility to leave for a young man with his own dreams and future."

He wiped his eyes. "I know you would be a great father. I want you to think about it. I have the papers here to sign if—"

Euphrates jumped up and interrupted Julian with a long-lasting hug. Euphrates took the paper from Julian and glanced through it. He snatched the pen out of Julian's pocket and he signed without hesitation.

Maurice thought to himself, *Euphrates must have anticipated something like this could happen.*

Julian added, "I discussed this with my dear Fina, and even though she has been so kind to be little J's surrogate mother, we both agreed that he needs a father, and you, Euphrates, are young and bright. You have a great future ahead of you. I want you to build a secure family that I've not been able to have."

Everyone at the table was wiping their eyes. Fina cradled Julian's hand between hers.

"Hey, this is a time to celebrate!" Julian exclaimed.

Maurice heard a quiver in Julian's voice and knew he was trying to lighten the mood and disguise his own emotions.

Fina interjected, "We're going to do our best that nothing happens to you, Julian. Maybe you should move somewhere safer, where they won't find you."

Julian shook his head. "Asilomar is my heart and soul. They found me here. They could find me anywhere, eventually."

Maurice looked at Euphrates, who, while saddened over Julian's pessimism, didn't seem all that surprised at what Julian had proposed.

Euphrates returned Maurice's gaze and smiled nervously. He clearly wasn't sure how this news would affect their young relationship.

Through the remainder of dinner, everyone was more quiet and reserved than usual. Euphrates brought out coffee and dessert. He had put on some soft jazz music in the background. It softened the edge created by Julian's announcement.

After they finished, Julian got up and put his arm around Euphrates and kissed both cheeks. Euphrates stood up, squeezed Maurice's shoulders, and then followed Julian into the house. They disappeared down the hallway.

Maurice looked at Fina.

"It's okay, Maurice. I'm sure they're going to spend some time together talking about everything. You know, Julian had mentioned this as a remote possibility to both Euphrates and me a while ago, so it didn't come as a great shock. It's just hard to accept. We never really thought it would come to this."

Maurice helped Fina clear the table and clean up the kitchen. He wanted to stay occupied for a little while.

He went outside to wipe down the dining table, when he noticed the guestbook was on one of the chairs. Julian must have left it.

He picked it up and looked around to see if anyone was watching. Not that it would have mattered, but the guestbook held a revered placed at Asilomar, and Maurice certainly didn't want to violate any special protocol.

He glanced through the ornately bound book and was careful not to crease any of the pages. He was slowly flipping through the pages and glancing at the various entries, when one in particular caught his attention. The name entered was "Clifford." Maurice straightened up and read the entry. "Legitimize my wanderlust."

"Oh my gosh!" he exclaimed. He quickly turned to see if anyone may have heard him.

Noticing that the date of his entry was only six months ago, he said to himself, "That has to be the same Clifford who I met in Madrid the day I arrived, and the water painting in my casita must be his too. What are the odds of that happening?"

He sat there for a moment with the guestbook open and recalled Julian's belief that "coincidence" rarely explains why someone is where they are supposed to be. He took a deep breath.

He quickly closed the guestbook, quietly walked into the house, and placed it on the kitchen counter. He returned to the patio and sat on the ledge overlooking the ocean, his favorite spot. It was dark, but the partial moon cast a rippling reflection over the water. Shaking his head, he was still mystified at how all the events of the past days were related and conspired to bring him to Asilomar.

He had been at Asilomar over two weeks, well past his original vacation schedule. Fortunately, he kept some income coming in from articles he'd write at night and e-mail the next day to his editor. He didn't know how much longer they would let him do this, but that wasn't his main concern right now.

He pulled the silver chain out of his T-shirt that had his medal medallion engraved with the Ithaca poem. It was joined by the silver hamsa that Euphrates gave him earlier in the day.

He knew his friendship with Euphrates had become more serious. Both were developing an emotional bond, and he understood that little J's guardianship added another level of complexity to a relationship that still had not been defined by either of them.

He clutched the chain in his hand. He thought about his first encounter with Claire, his unintended arrival at Asilomar, Julian and Euphrates, and now Clifford. He thought, *No, coincidence can't explain all of this.* The feeling of *saudade* that he experienced at the beach restaurant again overwhelmed him. He was content.

It was a day after Julian presented the legal papers relating to little Julian's guardianship that Maurice and Euphrates acted on their growing attraction to each other. That night, long after everyone had retired from dinner, Euphrates went to Maurice's casita and knocked on the door. Maurice was up late, as usual, writing notes that had accumulated in his head during the day.

He opened the door. "Hey, Euphrates, is everything okay?" As he rested his arm high on the door frame, his tank top pulled up, exposing the scar across his stomach that was now partly obscured by the curls of red hair that had grown back.

Maurice noticed Euphrates looking at his body and suddenly became conscious of the fact the he was wearing nothing under his loose shorts.

Euphrates was in a pair of long, baggy linen pants that were more like pajama bottoms and a loose-fitting tunic shirt. He didn't sign to Maurice or hand him a note. Instead he said one word and pointed to himself: "Pacha." He walked in the door and wrapped his arms around Maurice's waist and pulled him tightly against his chest.

Maurice said nothing and submitted to Euphrates's desires that night. As morning light arrived, the gentle breeze from the garden coming through the window blended with the sweet smell of their passion. They woke up with Maurice's arm across Euphrates's chest.

Over the next week, Euphrates and Maurice spent most of their time together, with the exception of when the entire household would gather for breakfast and dinner. They made sure they shared playtime with little Julian but would later find quiet places to enjoy one another's company.

Euphrates would usually go to the secret garden and work around the fountain. Maurice would sometimes climb over the patio wall and sit above the cliff, where he felt inspired to write. Their hikes down to the beach became almost daily excursions. Around four o'clock, when Fina, Julian, and little J were in siesta mode, they used that time to be alone and "talk." They would usually come back after an hour or so, shower, and get ready for dinner. The time spent together was invaluable in cementing their bond with one another. They shared no doubts about their physical attraction to one another. It was the emotional and spiritual bond that needed to be strengthened and shaped into a commitment of love and trust.

Occasionally they would spend an afternoon in the casita, lying on the bed, exchanging notes on their iPads. By sharing life stories and experiences, and triumphs and defeats, the bond between them grew closer. One afternoon they decided to share an experience that had a significant impact on their life. After about a half hour of writing on their iPads, they exchanged stories.

Maurice's story read,

> I was in my early twenties. I had come out later
> than most guys. I was returning one evening from

the convenience store near my apartment when suddenly, from out of a dark corner, two guys approached me. One of them walked right up to me and called me a dirty faggot. He yelled, "Get the hell out of our neighborhood!" Then he jumped on me and punched me in the stomach and face. I had wrestled in school, but he was much bigger than me, and before I knew it I was on the ground. When he started to kick me, his companion yelled, "Stop, Roman, stop! Enough!" The guy backed away, and the two ran down the street. I laid there for a few moments to catch my breath and regain my composure. My pride was wounded more than anything else. I got up and started to walk back to my apartment. I hadn't walked more than a block when a young man appeared from between two buildings. When he walked out beneath the street lamp, I recognized that he was the companion of the guy who beat me. Startled, I dropped the grocery bag and postured to defend myself.

The guy yelled, "Hey, man, it's okay. I'm not going to hurt you! I want to apologize for my brother. He's crazy and hateful. I didn't know he was going to attack you."

I didn't know what to say. For the first time I caught a good look at him. He was a handsome dude. He said, "My name is Cesar. Can I take you for a bite to eat? You know, to apologize for what happened?" It was probably against my better judgment but I said okay. At least I had the sense to suggest a place called Café Rosa, which was known to be gay friendly. I figured I would be safe there, and if he balked at the idea I'd know he wasn't sincere.

Well, it turned out he was gay, and we started dating. We were getting pretty serious. In fact, it was the first time another man had ever told me he loved me. But suddenly he stopped returning my phone calls. After nearly a month of no contact, he left me a voice mail message. He said his brother had seen us together and beat him badly. His brother also told his family about him, and they kicked him out of the house. He moved out of town to live with his cousin, and we never spoke again. Ever since that time, I've approached relationships with caution … and life, for that matter. When I think of that night I'm reminded of how love and violence can coexist—in the same place, in the same family, at the same time. Ever since then I get nervous when I start feeling close to someone, as if the other shoe to drop could be a violent one. I've been in love with the fantasy of falling in love but have never allowed myself to be in love…until now.

Maurice nervously twirled his fingers through his hair as he watched Euphrates read his long message. At certain points Euphrates would stop and frown. When he finished he wrote a note and handed it to Maurice. It read, "Is that why you were so upset after the guy attacked you and Julian?"

Maurice was surprised at how perceptive Euphrates could be.

Maurice wrote back, "Yes, the violence of that struggle along with the growing attraction I've had for you brought back those memories, and I started to withdraw for fear of being hurt again. I knew the situations were not the same, but I needed time to process it all."

Euphrates wrote back, "I will only fight to keep you. XO."
They exchanged a kiss.

It was Euphrates's turn. He handed Maurice his iPad and motioned for him to read.

I grew up in a small town in northern Spain. There were few Deaf people there, let alone the resources for us. In those days deafness was seen by many as an illness. To some people I was damaged goods. But my parents made sure I received the care and education I needed and sent me away to a special school for the Deaf. When I was in my late teens I knew what my orientation was, but I had few Deaf friends who were like me. There was one bar I would frequent. I was told I was attractive in an exotic way, as my background was different from most. But I discovered quickly that most guys only wanted me for sex. I didn't meet anyone who had the patience to take the time to know me as a person. I felt I had a lot to offer but began to doubt myself after a while.

Then I met Julian at the university and my life changed. He must have sensed something different about me, because he was the first person who really took an interest in me. He even learned sign language. His invitation to live at Asilomar was more than an act of kindness. I think he saved me from a life of self-doubt and despair.

Despite Julian's encouragement and the supportive spirit at Asilomar, I had all but given up on my own dream of falling in love. When you arrived I immediately found you attractive. I noticed when we made eye contact that you might have felt the same, but I was cautious too. I didn't want to get involved with someone who just wanted to mess around. My feelings changed when you asked if we had a sign language textbook. I was impressed, and after you defended Julian I knew you were special.

Maurice had been reading intently and was moved by Euphrates's story. He was struck by his spelling of the word *Deaf* with a capital *D*. Maurice recalled in his ASL lessons years ago that this usage indicated pride of Deaf culture and community. When he finished he rolled over and straddled Euphrates's lap. He ran both hands through Euphrates's curly hair. He cupped his face and kissed his forehead. The smell of cocoa butter lingered after their earlier walk on the beach. They lay there in an embrace until they fell fast asleep.

Landslide

*D*inner that evening had been routine. It was soon after everyone finished that Julian went inside to retrieve the guestbook. It had several colorful markers protruding from between the gold-edged pages.

Julian had been in a somber mood that evening. The atmosphere at Asilomar had become less peaceful and nurturing since the attack on Julian. The worry of more threats against Julian and his son was never far from their minds. Julian was showing the strain by not eating well. His face was gaunt, and he slept more than usual.

He paused and held the guestbook tightly with both hands. "Tonight I want to share a guestbook entry with everyone. This one is quite different from most."

He continued, "It's been well over five years since this guest visited Asilomar. At the time, as I'll explain shortly, I advised him how he might address his particular challenges. But it wasn't until these past couple of months that I really understood what he was experiencing. For this reason, it was important for me to revisit his guestbook entry and share it with those closest to me. Fina, would you be so kind as to pour some more wine for us?" Julian's voice wavered.

He continued, "This story concerns a retirement-aged gentleman from the United States who happened upon Asilomar in a unique way, as most guests have."

Julian took a sip of wine that Fina had placed in front of him. "A colleague of mine at the university called one day. He said there was a visiting student in his sociology class who didn't meet the typical student profile. First, he already had an advanced degree, and second, he was over fifty years old. But what captured my colleague's attention was the depth of discussion generated from the gentleman. While much of it was insightful to the class, there was also a troubling aspect that seemed deeply personal to the student. My friend thought he might find a couple of days at Asilomar, helpful in addressing some of what he called 'holes in his soul.'

"I agreed, and the man named Edward came to visit. Here's what he wrote in the guestbook: 'Landslide.'"

Julian paused and drank more wine.

"I asked Edward to tell me what 'landslide' meant. He explained it to me this way. Edward said that he had lost several close friends to the AIDS crisis in the 1980s. His wife passed away from cancer about that time, as well. He said for a long time his life was a recurring and painful cycle of hospitals, hospices, funerals, and memorials. It was like a whole chapter of his life had disappeared in a matter of a decade. He also had lost both parents.

"I recall Edward explaining that despite the joyful milestones in his life, the heavy burden of loss towered over him, and the pull of life's gravity sometimes created a landslide that buried him emotionally. He said it often felt like a part of him would slide into the ocean, leaving him feel less than a whole person. He confessed he would break down and cry in the middle of the day."

Maurice could hear Julian swallow as he continued. "The other day when I was going through the guestbook and came across Edward's entry, I was swept by a feeling similar to what he must have felt. I went on the patio and sat for over an hour trying to recall what my response to him was, hoping any advice I gave him could be helpful for me, as well.

"I recalled several things. First, I explained it was normal that memories from our past gurgle up to the surface and remind us of something joyful, painful, or just memorable. What matters is how we process those thoughts. Second, I said, you can't deny yourself the emotion that certain memories bring forward, good or bad, pleasant or painful. The memories are part of the process of living. The emotions that you feel indicate that you have been fortunate enough to have had a life full of rich human connections."

Julian looked down at the table and paused, as if he was reliving some past memories himself. "The universe has blessed me in so many ways, and while I've not experienced as much loss as someone like Edward has, I've seen the continuous burden of pain that many feel. We are all susceptible to landslides for any number of reasons."

He took a tissue out of his pocket and wiped his eyes. "I explained that while we are busy pushing and pulling our way through life, the universe has its way of giving direction. Sometimes it seems chaotic and not always to our liking, but it usually results in providing order in some form. There's an old Japanese proverb that says, 'The water flows but the river remains.'"

"I advised him to try something that I've been trying to do myself lately—compartmentalize. Think of your life as chapters in a book. Just because you've read them doesn't mean that the print has faded away. You can always reread them. Just visit each chapter individually as often as you wish or need."

Julian paused again to sip his wine. His face appeared strained as he recounted Edward's story. His eyes squinted and forehead wrinkled as he concentrated. It was as if Edward's story had become his own.

At that moment a cool breeze quietly swept through the patio, bringing with it a refreshing pause to Julian's emotional story.

He continued, "Edward commented how he wished he could rescript some of his past. I told him you can't redact life's past events.

If you're in search of the 'happily ever after,' it just doesn't exist. Celebrate that you were able to write those chapters in the first place. Many are not as fortunate. Think about how those who are gone would want you to live your life. Then think of the future as another compartment or chapter and how you want that story to be written."

Maurice felt Euphrates's hand squeezing tightly on his leg as Julian spoke. Fina had not taken her eyes off of Julian during the entire discourse.

Julian concluded, "I'm not sure exactly what impact our short time together had on Edward, but he did seem to leave with a lighter load on his shoulders. I can't minimize the effort it takes to negotiate this emotional terrain. I don't know if I did justice to Edward five years ago. I have to confess, following my own advice is a lot harder than I could have imagined.

"Edward sent me an e-mail last year that he had started a series of events at his home for friends and family. He called them 'Do Something' parties. As part of the invitation, each guest must bring a written promise of some act of kindness they will do over the next two months. At follow-up events he asked those same guests to share the act of kindness they performed. He started keeping a notebook of all of those events and has now published a book called *Doing Something*, which documents many of these acts of kindness. I understand his party idea has caught on in other cities. He told me he still has occasional landslides but that he got strength from believing he was living his life as those whom he had lost would want him to do."

Julian finally lifted up his head, tears running down his cheeks. "I was hoping that the memory of his visit would help me cope with my own landslide. For me it's not about a painful past but rather a future in which it's likely I may not see my son grow into manhood. I continually remind myself that it's the magic of the unexpected that often becomes the celebration of the extraordinary. It can be both good and bad. I can't see tomorrow from here, but we must embrace it when it comes."

Julian picked up his wineglass and walked to the edge of the patio and quietly stood there, looking out over the ocean. He turned back to look at everyone still seated at the table. He raised his glass. "I'm learning that we can't always fill the holes in our hearts, but we can repair and strengthen our souls. I love you all dearly."

Julian broke down, weeping loudly, as if weeks of pain were exploding from his chest. Fina, Euphrates, and Maurice rushed to embrace him. The rumble of Julian's personal landslide was felt throughout Asilomar that evening.

Kismet and Karma

*T*he following week at dinner, Julian suggested a short two-day trip to Granada. He explained, "I received a call from a former colleague of mine at the university. He asked if I would come and review some course proposals for him. I was thinking it might be good for all of us to get away for a change of scenery. Maurice, you could actually say you went to Granada, as planned!"

Maurice was excited that he finally would get to visit his alma mater. Euphrates, on the other hand, didn't seem to share the excitement, based on the rather solemn look on his face.

He signed something to Julian. Julian responded, "No, don't worry, Pacha. It's just for a couple of days. I'm feeling good, and Fina will take good care of little J. We can't hide in fear."

Euphrates shook his head back and forth. Maurice knew that Julian was going to do what he pleased despite his protests.

They decided to leave the next day.

Travel time to Granada was about three hours. The drive took them across the snowcapped Sierra Nevada mountains. They arrived early in the afternoon. They were only going to be there two nights. Julian suggested they first go to the campus of the university together. Julian could start his meetings, and Maurice could share his homecoming with Euphrates by touring the campus.

The remainder of the day went by fast. Maurice wasn't very

successful at finding anyone he had studied with but still enjoyed walking around the campus. Euphrates hadn't visited since his student days either, but he seemed less excited to be back.

The three had dinner together that night near the hotel, sharing accounts of what they did during the day. Tired from the drive and an afternoon of walking around the campus, they wrapped up the evening and retired to bed early.

The next morning Julian resumed his meetings, while Euphrates suggested to Maurice they go visit the caves on the edge of the city that were known for their flamenco shows. Originally, the caves were occupied by gypsies who helped develop the original style of dance.

They packed a little snack to take with them and headed on the highway out of town. Euphrates seemed to know where he was going. The air was warm and sweet. The sun's heat was intense as it poured through the open windows of the car. As they weaved their way through the narrow streets, Maurice couldn't stop looking up at the wrought iron balconies clothed in blooming pots and vines.

As they were driving, Maurice looked up toward the hills, recalling a tour to the flamenco caves he had taken as a student. It was the first time he had seen live flamenco dancing, and it was also where he had his first sexual experience.

It wasn't long before they were up to the area called Sacromonte, a location where the most well-known caves were located. A few of them still hosted flamenco shows; others were empty and open to the public for exploration.

Maurice was disappointed upon seeing how touristic the area had become in just the ten years since he was there. Souvenir booths lined the roadway, and gaudy billboards distracted from the natural beauty.

Euphrates shook his head and pointed farther up the mountainside. Euphrates kept driving another five minutes until the road had narrowed, ending in a dirt parking area. There were several cars parked there already.

Euphrates grabbed a few bottles of water out of the car. As usual he put his arm around Maurice's waist. They walked toward some rock formations partially obscured by brush and small trees.

As they got closer, Maurice could see the entrances to two small caves. He felt a little self-conscious with Euphrates at his side as he recalled the memory from his student days of an intimate moment with a young Spanish tour guide in the recesses of one of the caves. The guide had lured Maurice away from his student group just long enough to provide him his first sexual experience with a man.

Maurice quickly refocused his attention and walked closely at Euphrates's side. As they approached the caves, he was surprised to find an old man sitting outside collecting donations to enter.

At least there is not a booth selling souvenirs, he thought.

Maurice reached for some change in his pocket and paid the old man the small toll. Euphrates pointed to the cave on the left. He grabbed Maurice's hand and led him to the opening.

As they entered the cave, they were greeted by a rush of cool air. It felt refreshing in contrast to the warm temperature outside. The cave was dark, but some small lanterns inside provided enough light to follow the pathway. Maurice heard several voices, so he knew they weren't alone.

After walking for several minutes, Maurice saw a little recess that was hidden in the shadows. As they approached he felt Euphrates grab his arm and pull him into the darkness. Maurice pulled Euphrates close to his chest. He could feel the dampness of Euphrates's perspiration on the front of his T-shirt.

For a moment the caves were silent. The voices he heard earlier had faded. Euphrates put his moist lips to Maurice's ear. "I love you," he whispered.

Maurice replied by taking Euphrates's hand and putting it on his chest over his heart. They enjoyed a long, romantic kiss. Upon hearing the return of voices, Maurice released Euphrates from his tight embrace. He took his hand and led him back out to the main pathway, and they headed toward the daylight of the cave entrance. Maurice cherished that brief but romantic moment, much more so than his sexual initiation a decade earlier. As far as he was concerned, his visit there was complete.

The rest of the afternoon both men were simply happy to be in one another's company. They seemed to have connected on yet another level. Once back in Granada, they stopped at a small café located at the foot of the Moorish castle, Alhambra.

There was a small line of people waiting to be seated. Maurice went up to the hostess desk to ask the young girl to add him to the waiting list while Euphrates waited by the door. When Maurice turned around, he noticed a young man shoving Euphrates. He was dressed in business attire and carried a briefcase.

Maurice confronted the man, "Hey, excuse me. What are you doing?"

The man answered abruptly, "This jerk was standing in my way and wouldn't move when I asked him."

While he hadn't done so in a while, Maurice twirled his fingers in his hair. He responded, "He's deaf, sir. Please be patient and show some courtesy."

The man apologized to Euphrates.

Euphrates put his hand on Maurice's shoulder and signed that it was not a problem. He told Maurice that while these types of incidents are frustrating, he forgave people as long as they apologized.

Maurice was more upset than Euphrates, but he didn't want the incident to tarnish their romantic afternoon.

After enjoying a few tapas and some coffee, Maurice was still glowing inside from their walk in the cave. He suggested they go back to the hotel and relax. The shutters in their room opened to a view of the mountains. A large purple bougainvillea vine had made the climb to their second-floor balcony. They stripped down, crawled in bed, and fulfilled the promise of the kiss they shared in the cave.

At seven o'clock they joined Julian for dinner at the Rincón Criollo restaurant, where his friend Chef Ricardo worked. Julian had told Maurice that he was curious if Devin was still working there. Julian was in improved spirits and seemed rejuvenated from having spent some time reliving his past in academia.

When they entered the Rincón Criollo restaurant, they were greeted by a hostess. She wore a bright red dress with a laced top and had a traditional Spanish mantilla in her hair. She led them to a quiet table in the corner. Julian asked her if Chef Ricardo was working that evening. The lady excused herself and disappeared into the kitchen. Moments later a heavyset man wearing chef's whites came bounding out of the kitchen. When he saw Julian he exclaimed, "Hombre, it's so good to see you! I didn't know you were visiting. How have you been?"

Julian replied, "Everything is fine, Ricardo. You remember my friend Euphrates? And this is a special guest of ours at Asilomar, Maurice."

"Ah, yes, I remember Euphrates." They exchanged handshakes and smiled. "And nice to meet you, Maurice."

Julian interrupted, "Chef, I'm curious. Is that young man I introduced you to a couple of years ago still working here? His name was Devin."

Chef Ricardo beamed. "He is now my assistant executive chef. That fateful meeting at Asilomar was a blessing for both of us."

"Chef, I'm so happy it worked out … for both of you!" Julian's pride was evident from his broad smile.

The chef excused himself. "Julian, I'm sorry. We're very busy in the kitchen and I must get back. Have to make sure your dinner order is done to perfection!" He chuckled and hurried back to the kitchen.

Dinner was exceptional. They shared a sampler of meats and sausages typical of northern Spain. Euphrates signed that he was delighted with the restaurant, as it was reminiscent of the food he was accustomed to as a child.

Julian mentioned that his colleague had asked him to stay an extra day to be a guest lecturer in two of his classes.

"I was so flattered that Dr. Ortiz asked me to lecture for him. I wouldn't want to go back to full-time teaching again, but it would feel great to be back in a classroom again." Julian was signing to Euphrates in an excited fashion that Maurice hadn't seen before.

Julian added, "I want you guys to head back tomorrow. Dr. Ortiz said he'd provide transportation for me back to Asilomar the next day."

Euphrates shook his head. He signed something to Julian with a grimace on his face.

"Euphrates, don't worry. It will be okay. I'm here with a lot of friends. They'll make sure I have a ride back home."

They seemed to argue back and forth for a few moments. Julian signed without speaking, so Maurice wasn't sure what they were saying. He could tell from Euphrates's demeanor that he was not happy with Julian staying behind.

Finally, Euphrates signed as though he had given up and relented, but he still carried a frown on his face.

Maurice squeezed his leg for reassurance.

Midway through dinner a young man also wearing chef's whites approached the table.

"Julian, remember me? I'm Devin!" His chubby face was red, and sweat rolled down his cheeks.

"Of course I do!" A wide grin filled Julian's face as he held Devin's extended arm with both of his hands.

He continued, "Chef Ricardo tells me you are his assistant executive chef now. Congratulations! I'm so happy for you."

Devin graciously replied, "None of this would have been possible without you, Julian. None of it."

"I just led you to an open door, Devin. You walked through it."

Devin said hello to Euphrates and Maurice and then excused himself after explaining they had a private party they were preparing for.

As Devin left to go back into the kitchen, Julian looked at Maurice and said, "Maurice, what do you think?"

Maurice didn't hesitate. With a big grin he replied, "Devin is where he is supposed to be."

Julian laughed. "Ah, young warrior, you learned your lessons well."

The next morning Euphrates and Maurice met Julian for breakfast before their drive back to Asilomar. It was a little outdoor café around the corner from the hotel. They each had several espressos and some toasted bread with marmalade.

Euphrates signed in one last attempt to convince Julian to reconsider and come back with them.

Julian reassured him. "Euphrates, I'll be okay. Please don't worry, and enjoy your drive back."

Euphrates shrugged his shoulders.

As soon as breakfast was over, Julian wished them a good trip and they started on their way back to Asilomar.

The snow on the Sierra Nevada mountains that separated Granada from the Mediterranean Sea sparkled in the morning light. Maurice noticed that Euphrates was quiet and was still not happy about leaving Julian. After they drove for a while, Maurice recalled the good times they had in the cave. Euphrates squeezed his thigh and smiled.

In an attempt to make their field trip last a little longer, they stopped at a small café only a half hour outside of San Felipe.

At this point Maurice felt his sign language skills were progressing, and he was confident enough to sign to Euphrates and ask what he wanted to order.

Before long the waitress returned. First, she put a glass of wine and plate of chorizo and bread in front of Maurice. Unable to disguise her curiosity, she put a small plate with a little chocolate dessert in front of Euphrates and asked, "Is that all, sir?"

All of a sudden Euphrates started laughing. He tapped on the table and pointed at the lone brownie in front of him. He wrote a note to Maurice. "I wanted a beer, not a brownie! Back to LSE 101 for you!"

Maurice put his hands up to his face. "Oh my gosh. What did I do?"

Maurice's face turned as red as his hair. While the words "beer" and "brownie" were similar in LSE, they laughed about it the rest of the trip home.

When they finally arrived at Asilomar, Fina was sitting on the patio. Little J was pulling on Sucre's ears. She appeared to have had her fill of the little one's attention and ran up to meet the boys.

"Welcome back, boys. Did you have a good time?" asked Fina as she stood up and gave them each a generous hug.

"It was a very nice trip, Fina," responded Maurice. "But Julian wanted to stay another day. He was asked to be a guest lecturer for a colleague's class."

Euphrates's grimace returned.

Looking at the expression on Euphrates's face, Maurice added, "We tried to convince him to come back with us, but he insisted we go and that they'd provide a ride for him. He was really excited about being with students again. There was no way to convince him otherwise."

"Well, that's the stubbornness in Julian. I am happy that he's enjoying his trip." Fina went to the kitchen and came back with a tray of coffee and sandwiches.

"Ah, we're starving. Thanks, Fina," said Maurice as he rubbed his stomach and made a funny face at Euphrates.

While they finished their lunch, they gave Fina an account of their visit. They even described their special moment in the cave, which she could tell meant a lot to both of them.

Tired from the drive, Euphrates motioned to Maurice, who followed him inside the house and down the hallway up to his room. Maurice had been spending more time with Euphrates in his room and using the casita primarily for his writing.

They crawled in bed and cuddled up together, falling fast asleep.

The dinner chime sounded just as Sucre pushed Euphrates's door open. She put her head on the side of the bed closest to Maurice's face and whimpered. It was her signal it was time to get up.

"Okay, Sucre, we're getting up." They both laughed and slowly stretched away their sleepiness and headed down the stairs.

Fina had prepared a simple dinner. It included the red prawns that Maurice had such trouble negotiating on his first attempt. He broke through them like a pro this time. Euphrates shook his head in acknowledgment of his newly acquired prowess.

Maurice helped Fina clean up while Euphrates took little J out to the patio. When Maurice finished in the kitchen, he joined Euphrates. They pushed two lounge chairs together and nested little J between them. The little guy was chatty at first but soon fell asleep. Maurice thought he could hear the surf below. In a rare moment, his mind was empty of thoughts as he stared out into the darkness with the knowledge that there was a great ocean below.

Euphrates had already drifted off to sleep, when Fina came out and said, "Hey, boys. I need to put little J to bed. Can I get you anything?"

Maurice nudged Euphrates and signed if he wanted something to eat or drink. He shook his head.

Maurice replied, "Thanks, Fina. Go ahead and take the little guy. We can fend for ourselves here."

Fina took him in her arms, said good night, and disappeared into the house.

After a few minutes, Euphrates got up and went into the house. He was gone for about five minutes. When he came back out he had a book tucked under his arm. It was the guestbook.

He lit a small oil torch that was stuck in the ground at the edge of the patio.

Euphrates tapped Maurice's arm and handed him the guestbook. Maurice looked at him with an inquisitive face as Euphrates pointed to a blue marker near the front of the book.

Euphrates gave Maurice a handwritten note. "I've waited to share this with you because it is the most personal statement of who I am and who I want to be. I've never shared it with anyone before."

Maurice opened the book to the marked page. The entry read, "Euphrates."

He read it out loud to himself and paused between each of the five words that were written in Spanish: "*Nacer. Despertar. Imaginar. Sentir. Amar.*" In English it translated to "To begin. To awaken. To imagine. To feel. To love."

The profound simplicity of those five words laid bare Euphrates's life philosophy—his spiritual view of what his life journey should be.

Euphrates handed Maurice his iPad on which he had crafted a short note to better explain his guestbook entry.

It read,

I am a simple man. My journey from birth, to awakening and observing the world around me, to imagining my own destiny, to feeling and knowing the rainbow of emotions that fill a day from sunrise to sunset, and finally, to hoping to know love in an otherwise silent world. No, I cannot hear. But what the universe has taken from me it has given back twofold. The quiet that surrounds me only heightens my observations and sensitivity to everything around me. A beautiful and triumphant symphony— soundless but brightened by Asilomar's wondrous setting by the sea, by the loving and kind people in my life, and perhaps by a partner whose love for me may someday equal that which I have for him. I have my own dreams, but I also want to share in yours.

Maurice was overwhelmed by the fragrance of those words. He thought, *After all of my failed relationships, I happen to fall in love with a man who is unable to "listen" to me, but he "hears" me like no other person has.*

He held Euphrates's hand in a lasting grip. He knew that his new partner was complex and sensitive. He also knew that he wanted to share the journey with him.

They retreated to Euphrates's room for the night.

It was early morning. Maurice woke up with the soft glow of the sun filling the room. Euphrates was gone, but his side of the bed was still warm. Within a few minutes he returned to the room in his robe and leather sandals. He was carrying a tray of coffee and rolls. He tried to steal into the room unnoticed, but the spoons in the saucers had rattled on his way up the stairs.

Maurice was groggy but sat up and signed, "You would make a bad thief."

Euphrates laughed and set down the tray. He scribbled a short note to Maurice. "You just signed that I would make a bad cake!"

Maurice groaned and playfully rubbed Euphrates's curly hair. He found that trying to sign was more difficult for him than understanding someone else's signs. He needed a lot more practice but hoped that his signing skills would be advanced enough so that one day they could communicate effortlessly.

They enjoyed their coffee while sitting propped up against the pillows. The shutters were wide open, and there was a faint sound of the surf in the distance, enough to make Maurice stop and listen for a few seconds.

Euphrates tried to sign something, but Maurice was having trouble understanding. He reached for the pad of paper that he kept by his bedside for such occasions.

Euphrates wrote, "Something to show you outside."

Maurice nodded and finished the last of his coffee and signaled, "Let's go."

After slipping on T-shirts and jeans, they headed out to the patio where Fina was feeding little J. As soon as the little fellow saw Euphrates, he yelled out, "Oof, oof." Euphrates picked him up and twirled him over his head. He handed a note to Fina, asking if he was done eating so he could take him out in the garden with them.

Fina replied, "He's all yours. You guys try to wear him out for me, okay?"

Maurice laughed. "That's our job; don't worry."

Maurice followed Euphrates to what they now referred to as the "secret garden." Euphrates put little J down by the fountain and let him run around. He liked to chase the birds, but he would usually stumble and fall after a few steps.

Euphrates reached for Maurice's arm and pulled him to the "S" compass marker, where the tiles of Julian's initials were placed in the stone walkway. He motioned for him to walk counterclockwise around the fountain. They slowly passed the "E" marker and then paused at the "N" marker.

Little Julian was walking behind them but was having a difficult time staying upright on the uneven cobblestones.

Euphrates slowly guided Maurice a little farther to where his own initials, "EB," were placed. Maurice looked at him and shrugged his shoulders, not sure what point Euphrates was trying to make. Euphrates put his arm around Maurice's waist and led him to the "O" (for *oeste*, or west) marker. Maurice noticed that the patio had been broken up and repaired.

As they approached, Maurice yelled, "Oh my God, Euphrates!" He knelt down on the ground to get a closer look. Embedded in the patio were two tiles with his initials, "MS."

Euphrates's grin was so wide that his eyes squinted nearly shut, creating a road map of curves and dimples on his face. He looked down at Maurice and then pointed to the west in the direction of Las Vegas, Nevada, USA.

He uttered, "Yes, Las Vegas!"

Maurice jumped up and wrapped his arms around Euphrates. He didn't say anything more. It was unnecessary, as they were finding little ways to communicate their emotions toward one another.

Maurice loved to rub Euphrates's chest and gently pull on the dark curls that he knew would always be there. Euphrates rubbed his hand on the back of Maurice's head, burying his fingers in his red curls.

They had hardly any time to celebrate and enjoy the moment, when Maurice heard a scream and looked toward the house.

Maurice bolted toward the house. Euphrates picked up little J and followed as fast as he could.

Euphrates found Fina standing outside the kitchen door,

pounding the wall and crying. Euphrates was panicked, wanting to know what was wrong.

"Julian!" she screamed. She collapsed against Euphrates and hammered his chest with both fists. "He's dead!"

"They found him by the roadside on the outskirts of Granada. He'd been shot." Fina sobbed.

Euphrates had a confused look on his face and signed to Maurice, "What happened?"

He quickly scribbled a note on the pad of paper he kept in his back pocket. He held Euphrates's arm as he gave him the note.

It read, "Julian is dead. Someone shot him on his way back from Granada."

Euphrates lifted up his arms, almost knocking Maurice to the ground. He yelled something unintelligible, his hands slicing the air as if they were sharp knives. He bent over with his arms downward to the ground and then rose up quickly, as if trying to purge a painful monster trapped deep inside of him.

He came back to Maurice, who had his arms open to embrace him.

All three stood there, weeping and holding onto one another, as if one would fall without the other to hold him up.

The bad news that Julian had feared had finally arrived at Asilomar.

The sweet smells of the garden, the colorful palette of flowers, the fresh salty air coming off the ocean—none of this could disguise the pall of grief that hung over Asilomar those days that followed. Fina, Euphrates, and Maurice stayed close together but said little. At times one would start to cry, causing the others to begin to weep. It was a painful ring of fire that they had to pass through.

Their only joy now was little J, whose cheery face and bright disposition were free of the knowledge of what had just occurred.

He would sit in Euphrates's lap and stare at him and smile, almost as if to say, "It's okay, I'm where I'm supposed to be too."

They had spent almost an entire afternoon being interviewed by the Guardia Civil, or Spanish Police, about the incident. No one had been apprehended, and they had few clues as to whom the assailant might have been. While Fina and Euphrates had a good idea who was behind it, they could prove nothing. Even if they could have, they would have been reluctant to pursue it any further, as they feared retribution.

Fina and Maurice made arrangements for a funeral in Granada for later that week. Fina explained to the boys that Julian had at one time requested that he be cremated. They also planned to spend an afternoon signing paperwork at the Guardia Civil headquarters.

The drive to Granada was quite unlike the one Maurice and Euphrates had taken just days before. There was no laughter or excitement about visiting the city this time. Maurice drove, as Euphrates said he was still too upset to concentrate. He sat silently in the backseat, holding onto little J. He held him tightly by his side, as if he was trying to hold onto Julian's memory. Maurice would give an occasional loving look to the backseat to let Euphrates know that he was there for him but still allowing him his quiet time to grieve.

After a ride that seemed to never end, they arrived and checked into a hotel. Maurice made sure it was a different one from the one they had stayed at the week before. The memories of the three of them together were still too fresh. Maurice looked up toward the hills where the caves were. The natural beauty of Granada, the flowers, and the distant snowcapped mountains appeared colorless, as if he was looking through gray gauze.

Maurice took care of making most of the funeral arrangements. Although it would be a very private ceremony, Euphrates contacted a few of the university staff and professors who knew Julian. Before they left Asilomar, Maurice had tried a number of times to call

Claire but could only get her voice mail. He left a message that it was urgent. He had yet to hear back from her.

Once they had made the arrangements, they did nothing but sit around the hotel. Nobody felt like venturing out, though they did have dinner at an outdoor restaurant around the corner.

"Let's get a couple bottles of wine, okay? I think we all need some liquid courage," Maurice suggested.

Maurice tapped Euphrates on the shoulder to get his attention. He had drifted off, staring at the fountain across from them. Maurice held up the wine list and pointed with two fingers. "Two bottles." Euphrates nodded his agreement.

The wine helped to take the edge off. They tried to talk about Julian in a more celebratory way—what he had accomplished for himself and for others. Euphrates went through almost a whole tablet of paper, expressing the feelings he had kept bottled up inside. He wrote of his joy when Julian first invited him to Asilomar, and when little J was born. He spoke with sorrow about the tragic death of Julian's wife. The final note that he handed to Maurice said, *"Nacer, despertar, imaginar, sentir, amar"* (To begin, to awaken, to imagine, to feel, to love). He circled the word *"sentir"* (to feel).

Shortly after they returned to their hotel rooms, Maurice's phone rang. It was Claire. Her voiced crackled with nerves.

"Hello, Claire."

"Hi, Maurice. I just got your message. What's happening?"

"Claire, Julian has been murdered."

A few seconds went by with no response on the other end.

"My God, I always worried so about my Jules. I think he knew it would end this ..." She couldn't finish.

Maurice gave her a few moments. He later explained a few more details of what happened and gave her the information about the service. Naturally, Claire wouldn't be able to join them but said she would have flowers sent to the chapel.

"How are you boys and Fina doing?" she asked.

"The best we can." Maurice nervously ran his hand through his hair.

"What about little Julian? Is he okay?" Claire inquired.

Maurice replied, "Yes, he's safe and sound." He paused for a moment and then continued, "Claire, I don't know if you knew, but Julian had prepared some legal papers giving Euphrates custody of him. It's as if he knew this was coming."

Claire said, "No, I didn't know, but I think he did sense something could happen, Maurice. I think he did."

After offering any assistance she could provide from afar, Claire said good-bye. She said that she would call them after the funeral service.

Julian had once told Fina that he would never want a religious ceremony, but they all thought that the university chapel would be a nice place to hold the service. It was small, with simple decor, and not overwhelmed with crucifixes and statues of the Virgin Mary, which they knew meant little to Julian.

The service was held the next morning. In front of the small altar was a wooden stand. Sitting on top was a small silver urn that contained Julian's remains. It was plain, with no design or writing on it. Moments before the service, a young man entered the chapel and placed a vase of orange and yellow daylilies by the foot of the stand. Maurice leaned over and took a peek at the attached envelope. It was from Claire. He took the little floral card with Claire's name on it and passed it to Euphrates and Fina.

Fina whispered back, "Daylilies were some of his favorites. Claire knew." She offered a faint smile.

The service lasted only fifteen minutes. At Euphrates's request there were no eulogies, just silent remembrances. A university chaplain gave a short sermon about the celebration of life. About a half-dozen of Julian's colleagues attended.

Fina had requested that a recording of the second movement of Rodrigo's *El Concierto de Aranjuez* be played at the end of the service. The melodic and deliberate guitar work displaced their pain with a sense of quiet regret. Euphrates turned and signed to Maurice asking him to describe what the *Concierto* sounded like. Maurice was deeply affected by the music and had to think for several minutes. Then he wrote on his note pad, "It's like the invisible caress of a cloud brushing across your cheek, and the tickle of pebbles tumbling over your feet in a cool stream." Although it was a silent moment for Euphrates, the tearful response on his face was apparent to Maurice.

After the ceremony, Maurice handed Euphrates the jar containing Julian's ashes. Euphrates held it for a moment and then gave it back to Maurice, motioning for him to hold onto it for now. Euphrates reached down and picked up little Julian. The two had been nearly inseparable the past few days. Before he left the chapel, Euphrates picked one of the daylilies from Claire's flower arrangement and put it in his pocket.

They left early the next morning to head back to Asilomar. While exhausted from the stress, Maurice encouraged Euphrates and Fina to focus on celebrating Julian's life and accomplishments. Fina recalled some of the fond memories she had with Julian, but Euphrates quietly sat in the backseat, holding little Julian during the entire trip.

After arriving, they each went to their rooms to shower and change. Maurice didn't know what to do with the silver urn, so he placed it temporarily in a little cubbyhole in the outside wall by the patio. A friend of Fina's had prepared a large pan of paella with chicken and rabbit so they didn't have to cook.

Euphrates brought out a few bottles of wine. Their ravenous appetites emptied the paella pan. Dinner was followed by coffee and a tray of churros that they bought on the road.

Maurice joked, "I've never eaten so many churros in my life!"

His comment was enough to prompt a much needed giggle from Euphrates and Fina.

It wasn't quite dark yet. Maurice motioned to Euphrates to follow him out to the secret garden. Maurice walked over to the cubbyhole and grabbed the urn. He took Euphrates's hand and led the way to the garden and around to the compass. He placed the urn by Julian's initials. Euphrates acknowledged his approval by squeezing Maurice's hand.

They remained there for a few moments in silence and then walked back to the patio.

As usual, Maurice spent the night with Euphrates, but neither felt playful. They curled up close, falling asleep, comforted by one another's warmth.

Over the next several days, everyone had a difficult time trying to get back to life as usual. After all, what was usual now? They felt awkward in attempting to resume any form of routine. The vacuum left by Julian was great. It was as if some of the oxygen had been removed from the atmosphere. Everyone felt it.

Yard work, house chores, and beach excursions had become necessary distractions for Euphrates and Maurice.

Early one morning there was a knock on the door. Someone yelled, "Is anybody home?"

Maurice was in the kitchen and heard the strange voice.

Sucre's bark had also alerted Maurice that someone was there. Still nervous about the previous intrusion, Maurice cautiously approached the door and looked through the little latch to see who it was.

"Who is it?" inquired Maurice.

"I'm an attorney representing Mr. Julian Bakkar," the voice said.

Maurice had a difficult time making out the figure through the little opening.

"I have a legal document that pertains to Mr. Euphrates Baroja and Ms. Fina Echeverria," the man added.

Maurice slowly opened the door. The visitor was wearing a dark suit, white shirt, and tie and carrying a brown briefcase. He looked and acted very businesslike.

Maurice stood silently staring at the man, wondering if he was legit.

"May I come in?" he inquired.

"Uh, do you have some form of identification?" Maurice asked, thinking he couldn't be too careful.

The gentleman reached into his suit pocket and presented Maurice with his business card. It read, "Enrique Castro, Attorney, Castro, Ruiz & Associates."

"Thank you. Come in," Maurice said in a less-than-enthusiastic tone.

He led the man through the entryway out to the patio.

Fina was mending some clothes on the patio. Euphrates was in the garden playing with little J.

Maurice invited the man to sit down and offered him some coffee.

Maurice explained to Fina, "This gentleman is an attorney, and he says he has some documents for you and Euphrates."

Fina's eyes opened wide.

"Here's his business card, Fina." Maurice handed her the card.

Fina said, "Hello, Mr. Castro. I'll get some coffee. Maurice, Euphrates is out in the garden with little J. Would you call him, please?"

Maurice picked up a ball that Sucre played with and threw it in the yard toward Euphrates. As the ball rolled by him, he looked up and Maurice motioned for him to come in.

Euphrates picked up little J and held him up on one of his shoulders as he headed back to the house.

Fina returned with a tray of coffee.

Euphrates grimaced upon seeing the man in a dark suit sitting at the table.

He put little Julian down and approached the table. He looked at Maurice, who handed him a note.

"Mr. Castro, an attorney, has papers for you and Fina."

Euphrates turned to the attorney and then back to Maurice. Maurice shrugged his shoulders, indicating that he had no idea what it concerned.

Euphrates sat down while the man opened his briefcase and pulled out a blue folder with some papers in it. The attorney started to converse with Euphrates, when Maurice interrupted.

"Mr. Baroja is deaf," Maurice explained. "Please speak slowly so he can see your lips. I'll write the important information on paper for him."

The attorney proceeded. "I represent the estate of Mr. Julian Bakkar."

Maurice jotted down notes for Euphrates as fast as possible. The matter was too serious to risk using his signing skills.

The attorney looked at Euphrates, who nodded that he understood.

"Mr. Bakkar's will has been submitted to my firm. These papers summarize his final wishes."

The attorney spoke in a monotone voice. The coldness of his presentation sent a chill through Maurice.

Euphrates looked at Maurice for an explanation. Maurice quickly wrote a note on paper.

Euphrates read it and nodded to proceed.

The attorney asked both Fina and Euphrates for identification. Fina had it in her purse. Euphrates had to run upstairs to get his passport.

After Euphrates returned and their identities were confirmed, the attorney opened the blue folder and shuffled through some papers. He pulled out two formal-looking documents and placed one down in front of Fina. He kept the other for himself.

He ran his finger down one of the pages and stopped at one of the paragraphs in the middle. He directed Fina to a little sticky note on her copy, highlighting the same paragraph. He read, "To Fina Echeverria, I leave $50,000 in cash." He stopped reading.

Fina gasped, clutching her throat. "I had no idea!" she exclaimed. Maurice hurriedly scribbled a note and handed it to Euphrates. Euphrates read the note explaining Fina's inheritance. Maurice saw the look of amazement on Euphrates's face as he turned to Fina and nodded.

Next, the attorney pulled a similar-looking document out of the folder and handed it to Euphrates. Again, he looked for the appropriate paragraph and directed Euphrates to the correct place on his copy.

He read aloud, "I assign Euphrates Baroja as trustee of a fund for Julian Bakkar Jr., my son, for whom Mr. Baroja is now trustee and guardian. The trust is in the amount of $100,000 to be used for making sure he grows up to be the man we all wanted him to be; I also request that it be used in part for his advanced education, as seen fit by Mr. Baroja."

Euphrates remained motionless.

The attorney pointed to another paragraph on the same page and read it aloud. "To Mr. Baroja I separately leave $50,000 in cash."

The attorney paused.

As Euphrates read along, his jaw dropped and his mouth hung wide open. Maurice tapped on the table. Euphrates looked up and kept shaking his head back and forth.

The attorney said that there was more and pointed to the last page of Euphrates's document.

He read aloud, "To Mr. Euphrates Baroja I leave the property known at Calle del Mar Vista 1, San Felipe, also known as 'Asilomar.'"

Euphrates's head sagged even farther, and tears began to stream onto the table. Maurice rushed over to hold him. It took several minutes for him to stop crying.

The attorney motioned to Euphrates and Fina and added, "There is one more paragraph I need to read."

He turned a page on his copy and opened Euphrates's copy to the paragraph marked by a red sticky note. Once they found it, the attorney continued to read aloud. "To the best of their ability, I ask my loved ones to scatter my ashes in the ocean at the entrance to the Caves of Hercules in Morocco."

The attorney paused and then asked with a near expressionless face, "Do you have any questions? If not, that is all I have for you today."

Maurice looked at Fina and Euphrates in case they had questions. They were both still too stunned to respond.

The attorney asked them each to sign their copy. He asked Maurice to sign as a witness to each of their documents, as well. He explained it would take up to four weeks for the courts to process the will.

Euphrates reached over and picked up little J and hugged him so tight that the little one let out a squeal like a baby pig.

Maurice was escorting the attorney to the door when the gentleman stopped suddenly and said, "Oh my, I almost forgot. I have two envelopes that were sent to our office not long ago with instructions to attach them to Mr. Bakkar's will. One is addressed to Ms. Fina Echeverria and the other to Messrs. Baroja and Summerlin."

Fina was the first to open the envelope. Her short plump body shook as she read to herself the note that was written in Julian's handwriting.

My dearest Fina,

I know I was never able to fulfill the role as husband to you, but I love you deeply. You were the voice of reason to my unbridled passions. I love you dearly. I'm confident your spirit will keep you strong. Always know that I'm with you.

Love, Julian

Maurice and Euphrates stood on either side of Fina. She wilted in their arms. They sat her on a chair for a few moments until she regained her composure.

She handed them the note to read.

After reading it, Maurice hugged her and Euphrates gave her a kiss on the forehead.

It was their turn to open the other envelope. Euphrates motioned for Maurice to proceed.

Maurice slid his finger under the seal and took out the small handwritten note. Maurice held the note while they both read it together.

Dearest Pacha and Maurice,

My favorite quote from Lao Tzu encourages me to believe that you will grow to become the loving partners that I know you're capable of becoming. "Being deeply loved by someone gives you strength, while loving someone deeply gives you courage."

I wish you strength and courage. I love you both,

Julian

As if the reading of the will wasn't enough, the emotions generated by Julian's notes left the three of them broken.

Fina quickly showed the attorney to the door and rejoined Maurice and Euphrates, who were still standing frozen in shock in the hallway.

Maurice put his arms around Fina and Euphrates and pulled them tightly against his short frame. There were no words that needed to be spoken.

After two weeks, Maurice still had to keep reassuring Euphrates that Asilomar was his, or would be shortly. Euphrates expressed disbelief to Maurice that it was really happening. He said that while Julian's old room downstairs was much larger, he wanted to continue to live in his room. He told Maurice that it would take time to fill the empty hole in his heart left by Julian's absence. He was rarely seen without little J in his arms. Maurice had become a surrogate second father, such that the little one was starting to mumble "Mauu mauu."

After some discussion, Euphrates and Maurice made plans to fulfill Julian's wishes and take his remains to Morocco. It was a four-hour drive south to the port of Algeciras, where they would catch a ferry across the Strait of Gibraltar to Tangier. The Caves of Hercules would be a thirty-minute cab ride from there.

On the two-hour ferry ride, Euphrates didn't say much. He wore the most traditional Moroccan clothes that he had—a full-length tunic, a head scarf, and his orange Moroccan leather slippers. Tucked away inside his tunic was the small urn that he clutched tightly the entire trip. It was a clear but windy day, and the rough seas were making the ferry heave from side to side. Maurice was feeling a little woozy but did his best not to be the spoiler for this special day. They didn't say much during the crossing. Euphrates stood by one of the ship's railings and stared out to sea.

Upon arriving they hailed a taxi for the short ride to the caves. There were several legends associating Hercules to the caves; one was Greek and the other was Roman. One suggested that he lived in the caves before he did his eleventh labor. The other purported that Hercules had to cross a great mountain called Atlas. Using his legendary strength he broke through the mountain and joined the Atlantic Ocean with the Mediterranean Sea. The mountain peaks on either side of the strait between Spain and Morocco came to be known as the Pillars of Hercules.

Euphrates told Maurice that he would like to think that because of his ability to cut through people's doubts and fears, it was the second legend that would have appealed to Julian.

It was a popular tourist attraction regardless of which legend one found appealing. They were pleased to find a smaller-than-expected crowd at the caves. They asked the taxi driver to wait, knowing they would not be any longer than fifteen or twenty minutes.

They walked down to the entrance of the cave, trying to get as close to the water as possible. While it was a clear day, there was a heavy mist rolling ashore from the high surf. They scrambled over slippery stones, as there was no clear pathway to the water. High tide made it possible not to have to walk too far out on the jagged rocks that fronted the cave. When Euphrates felt he was in a secure spot, he pushed aside his flowing tunic. Maurice noticed his hand was red from clutching the urn so tightly. Euphrates reached out with the other hand to bring Maurice close to him.

Euphrates pulled a wrinkled piece of paper out of his pocket and handed it to Maurice. On it he had scribbled a short quote from one of his favorite musicians, Jimi Hendrix. He explained to Maurice before they left that it was ironic Hendrix had written it shortly before he died in a London hospital. Balancing on the rocks with Maurice's help, Euphrates slowly opened the urn. Maurice read the quote: "The story of life is quicker than the wink of an eye, the story of love is hello and goodbye until we meet again."

Euphrates slowly poured the white powder of what remained

of Julian into the sea. As the last grain of it emptied from the urn, Maurice said, "I love you, Julian." Euphrates signed the same.

This time they had no tears but rather embraced in celebration of having known such a great and generous man.

They rejoined their waiting taxi driver and began the long journey back to Asilomar.

Dreams to Pursue

As they opened the front gate, Sucre ran up to greet them.

"Hi, girl. It's always good to see my little lady." Maurice got on his knees to embrace Sucre. He looked up at Euphrates and signed, "Are you hungry?"

Euphrates nodded but pointed to the upstairs, indicating he wanted to shower and change.

Maurice left to go to his casita, where he still kept his clothes. He wanted to clean up as well.

As he passed through the kitchen, he encountered Fina sitting at the table with little J in her lap. She looked tired.

"Hello, *hijo*. Did everything go all right?" Little Julian was hitting Fina playfully, but she kept pushing his hands away from her face.

Maurice grabbed him and put him on the floor. He stood over Fina and gently massaged the back of her neck. "Yes, it was quite a long trip … the car, the ferry, the taxi. But the experience at the cave was something neither of us will ever forget. I think Julian would have been happy."

Fina nodded and rubbed Maurice's arm. "I don't think I could have endured another emotional moment. I'm glad you guys are back though. It was lonely here today without you."

She continued, "I know you boys are probably hungry. I didn't get around to preparing a dinner, but I thought we could make tapas tonight. Does that sound okay with you?"

Maurice was delighted. He loved tapas, and it would be less formal than a dinner. They all needed to chill out. "Yes, that's perfect, Fina. Let me shower and clean up, and I'll help you out in the kitchen."

With all the drama and tragedy that had occurred, Maurice temporarily had lost touch with Asilomar, "the place." But as he walked back to the casita, he suddenly became more aware of his surroundings again. The flowers were still brilliantly showing off their colors, the air was scented by the dampness of the ocean, and huge white cumulus clouds were floating above. He thought that, despite all the changes that had happened, the natural beauty and spirit that was the foundation of Asilomar had remained constant and consistent. He felt comforted.

Maurice sat on the steps of the casita for a few moments to take it all in.

He showered and put on some fresh clothes. Before leaving to go back to the house, he sat on the edge of his bed to tie his tennis shoes. As he looked up, his eyes were drawn to the little framed watercolor on his wall. He stared at the signature in the lower right-hand corner. A broad smile spread across his face as he viewed the evidence of Clifford's artistry as another sign that at this moment, this was where he was supposed to be.

Maurice returned to help Fina prepare the tapas. Little J was happily playing on the floor with some large spoons that Fina had given him.

"Okay, now what are we doing here?" he asked Fina. "I'm your trainee."

Fina laughed and responded, "It's going to be simple. I'm making four different tapas: a fried potato omelet with eggs, ham and shrimp croquettes, cubes of chicken on a skewer, and slices of chorizo with fresh bread."

"Hmm, sounds fantastic. What can I do?" Maurice was more interested in tasting than helping, but he was still curious about how she prepared the tapas.

"I've already cut everything up. You could put the chicken on the skewers and add a couple of pieces of onion and mushroom on each one. It's really simple, but I'm enjoying your company." Maurice joked as he skewered the chicken.

Euphrates knocked on the wall as he entered the kitchen to avoid startling them.

He picked up little J and gave him a big kiss and set him back on the floor.

He gave Maurice a hug from behind. Maurice picked up a piece of chorizo and teased him with it. Euphrates opened his lips as Maurice put the piece of chorizo in his mouth.

"You boys better not eat everything before I get a chance to get it all ready." Shooing them away playfully, she continued, "Why don't you sit down and relax. I'll be out in a minute. Euphrates, you could get the wine ready." She pointed to the bottle of red wine on the counter.

Euphrates opened the bottle, and Maurice grabbed three glasses. They went out to the patio with little J following behind. Sucre decided to stay close to Fina, knowing she would probably get treated to some chorizo and ham.

When Fina brought out the tapas, Euphrates filled each glass halfway with wine. As they sat there looking at the food, there was a collective sigh. Euphrates reached both arms across the table and grabbed Maurice's and Fina's hands. He gave them both a big squeeze. Maurice then sat up and raised his glass of wine. They did, as well.

"May your journeys be long, and may your dreams be forever. *Salud.*" Maurice led the toast.

After a few moments of sampling the tapas, Fina said with some worry in her face, "You know there have been some cars driving up the hill and turning around lately. I don't know if it's just folks who are lost or what. I guess I'm super nervous now."

Fina wrote a note for Euphrates at the same time she was talking.

Even though Maurice was getting more proficient in signing, they were still going through a lot of paper without Julian around to interpret.

Maurice asked, "How often have you seen them? Is it always the same car?"

Fina shook her head. "Not every day. Sometimes I don't see anything. I just hear the car."

Euphrates pulled little J off the floor and put him in his lap, as if he sensed danger.

"Let's hope they're just lost," lamented Fina.

They were too tired to worry and hoped to convince themselves that Fina was right.

Maurice and Euphrates cleaned up so Fina could relax and put little J to bed.

Everyone was exhausted, so they made it an early evening. This time, however, Euphrates signaled to Maurice to go to the casita. He wrote Maurice a short note: "I don't want to sleep in the house tonight." Maurice nodded, knowing that he had not been sleeping well upstairs because of bad dreams. *How ironic*, Maurice thought— *Asilomar*, the place of dreams. They slept soundly that night

Later that week Maurice's boss sent him a message saying they couldn't hold his job for him much longer. In the past month he had only submitted a few stories for the magazine and recently began to live off of his savings. He wrote an e-mail to his boss thanking him for his patience but informed him that he would not be returning.

Euphrates told him not to worry. He wanted him there with

him, and there was nowhere else Maurice could have imagined he would want to be.

Over the next two weeks, Maurice and Euphrates fell into a predictable routine of working in the garden and playing with little J in the morning. Every couple of days after lunch, they would walk into town with Fina to get supplies. If they had a lot of things to get they would drive, but usually they preferred to walk. Little J loved riding on Euphrates's shoulders on the way down the hill. Going uphill they would trade off carrying him and then usually stop by the old windmill to rest.

On one trip they stopped as usual at the windmill. Euphrates took Little J around the back to show him the bushes of wild raspberries that amazingly defied the arid climate and poor soil. Alone for a few moments, Maurice stood in the doorway of the windmill. Once again the feeling of *saudade* overtook him. He looked up and thought, *How ironic that in an iconic structure that symbolizes illusion and delusion, I finally feel clarity and a sense of purpose.*

When Euphrates and Little J returned, Maurice pulled some coins out of his pocket and threw them in the water trough, as was the custom. At that moment a strong breeze whipped down the hillside. A loud creaking sound above them caught Maurice's attention. The blades of the quixotic windmill, stripped of its ancient sails, had moved slightly, as if waking from a deep sleep. *A sign,* he thought, *that maybe I am following the right path.*

On the days they didn't go into town, Euphrates and Maurice would hike down the cliff to the beach. They still looked forward to this time together. They loved Asilomar, but the beach allowed them to disconnect from all the reminders of the things that had transpired. Bringing a bottle of wine, bread, and cheese or chorizo had become their tradition.

One afternoon as they sat on the blanket staring out at the ocean, Euphrates tapped Maurice on the shoulder. He signed that he wanted to walk along the water's edge. They rolled up their jeans and took off their shoes and socks. It was a warm afternoon, and the water felt refreshing as it washed up over their feet.

As usual, they found themselves alone on the beach. They held hands and walked slowly, as if they had no particular destination in mind. As they reached an outcrop of rocks, Euphrates led Maurice to the top of one of the large boulders.

Euphrates reached in his jeans and pulled out the paper and pen he always carried. He wrote, "Did Julian die so we could pursue our dreams?"

Maurice thought for a few moments and then responded with a longer note. "I don't know. For certain I believe his dream of a better life for little Julian will be fulfilled through us. I think it also may have given us an opportunity as a couple, to move on and build a life for ourselves."

Euphrates squinted and looked troubled. He took the pad of paper from Maurice and scribbled, "But not here. Asilomar is not good anymore."

At first Maurice was surprised. It sounded out of place for anyone to describe Asilomar as bad, especially Euphrates. Maurice would have been willing to help Euphrates continue Julian's work if he wanted to, but he knew it was probably wise to leave.

Euphrates wrote another short note. "We need to leave to save little J."

Maurice agreed that Asilomar had changed, or at least the world around it had. He signed, "Yes, I understand." He put his arm around Euphrates, and they slowly walked back down the beach to their blanket.

Dusk was approaching. The seams on the horizon that bound the sea and the sky together became animated with rapidly changing colors—pale blue, to orange, to pink, and then purplish gray, ultimately fading as the daylight dimmed to where there was no longer a horizon. The mountains that earlier were multidimensional and textured with crevices and ridges slowly transformed into dark silhouettes. As they watched the unstoppable arrival of nightfall, their heavy hearts sensed that perhaps the sun was setting on Asilomar, as well.

The next morning Fina ran out to the patio with an unmarked envelope in her hand.

She saw Euphrates working in the garden. Maurice was nearby lying in the grass, playing with little J. She threw Sucre's ball again at Euphrates to get his attention. He looked up and saw Fina waving him to come back to the house.

Euphrates stood there for a few seconds. He dropped the clippers and walked over to Maurice and pointed to where Fina was standing.

Maurice picked up little J, and they met Fina at the patio.

She was breathing heavily but explained, "I heard Sucre barking out front and found this envelope laying at the front door. I heard a car heading down the hillside." Maurice turned to look at Euphrates as a bad feeling once again overcame him.

Fina was afraid to open the envelope and handed it to Euphrates. He hesitated and gave it back to Maurice.

Maurice opened the envelope and slowly pulled out a small yellow piece of paper with a short message. It was typed but with several misspellings. He read it aloud as Euphrates looked over his shoulder.

"Son of Julian need to be returned to his rightful famly. He must be surendered to us or we take him by force."

The note went on to say that they were to bring Little J to the port in Algeciras, which was across the channel from Tangier, two weeks from that day.

Euphrates dropped the paper on the patio floor. His stunned

look was soon replaced by an angry frown. He signed wildly, as he had done before when he was upset. He shook his head and said as loud as he could, "No, no, no!"

Maurice reached down, read the note, and looked at Fina. "I assume they are referring to the family of Julian's deceased wife?"

Fina nodded.

Euphrates picked up little Julian in his arms and held him tight to his chest, shaking his head and mumbling in a softer voice, "No, no, no."

For the rest of the day they stayed inside the house. Euphrates and Maurice spent the rest of the morning up in his room with little Julian on the bed with them. Fina stayed busy in the kitchen preparing dinner. Euphrates told Maurice he had no appetite and didn't want any lunch. Maurice took little J downstairs for his snack.

"Fina, Euphrates wants to leave Asilomar," said Maurice.

"I know. I can see it in his face. And you know, I think he's right. I don't want the same thing that happened to Julian to happen to either of you. And you both have to do whatever it takes to protect the boy. Julian believed in both of you."

Maurice nodded. "I know you're right. I'm going to leave him alone for a while upstairs, but I think we need to talk about this at dinner tonight."

Fina rubbed Maurice's head and brushed back his red curls. "I know you boys will do the right thing."

Dinner that night carried a sense of foreboding. The atmosphere seemed empty of the usual sound of night birds singing. The gentle ocean breeze that one could count on to carry in a salty scent was absent.

Euphrates was carrying out his usual task of pouring the wine while Fina and Maurice brought out the food, a seafood paella of shrimp, crab, mussels, octopus, and fish. It had kept Fina occupied in the kitchen for most of the day.

Maurice started to raise his glass to make the usual toast. Euphrates held up his hand to stop Maurice. He handed Maurice a note and signaled him to read it. It was a new toast.

Maurice read, "May our journeys now take us to where we are supposed to be. *Salud*."

During dinner, Euphrates exhausted an entire pad of paper writing down suggestions for what they should do. He proposed going to northern Spain, where his family was from. Fina convinced him that they would find the three of them there, as well.

Fina shared her desire to reopen her pastry shop. With the money Julian left her, she could live comfortably without having to work so hard. She loved her little village of San Felipe, and now she could afford to get better medical treatment for her sister Elena too. The boys agreed.

Euphrates continued to write down suggestions, such as moving to England or even farther, maybe Japan. He thought of living on a sailboat or buying a small island somewhere. Frustrated, he put his pad down and sat with his head in his hands.

Maurice moved his chair close to Euphrates and rubbed his neck.

Fina wrote Euphrates a note. Maurice read it over his shoulder. "You'll need to find Julian an environment where he can get a good education and make friends and have a real childhood."

Euphrates pointed to Fina, acknowledging that she was correct.

Maurice reached over and handed him a note, as well. It said, "We will find the right journey, Pacha. I know we will."

Over the next several days, the three of them were busy closing up Asilomar. Euphrates shared his sadness with Maurice that this once lush and colorful garden would slowly wither without water and care. He drained the plumbing to the fountain.

Maurice was busy helping Fina put kitchen materials away and packing up food that they would take to her house in town.

Fina made some lemonade and filled two glasses. "Here, Maurice. Take one to Euphrates. I worry that he's working too hard out in the heat today. Poor fellow, I know this breaks his heart too."

Maurice grabbed the glasses and went out by the casitas where Euphrates was busy securing the shutters closed and nailing boards across the doorways.

As Maurice approached, he stopped for a brief moment and watched Euphrates pick up a two-by-four and nail it across a doorway. He was dripping wet from the heat. The moisture in his short curly hair formed beads liked crystal ornaments. On his face there were droplets running down his cheeks, but they weren't all because of the heat.

Maurice handed him a glass of lemonade and signed him to come back to the house.

Maurice led him to the ledge at the end of the patio. They sat there looking out over the expanse of blue sea, as they had done countless times before.

Maurice felt Euphrates's arm wrap tightly around his waist. The understanding that they needed and wanted one another had never been so strong. He thought, *I'll never be the old version of myself again.*

Homecoming

"Uncle Morris, wake up, wake up!" The little twelve-year-old boy was tugging at his pant leg. Jonas was a bright and inquisitive young boy. He shared his father's dark complexion and curly black hair.

"Whaaat? Whaaat?" murmured the man still half-asleep on the chaise lounge. He rolled over and opened his eyes.

"Uncle Morris, Papa says you need to get ready. It's getting late, he says." The little man waved his arms and motioned with his hands to emphasize the urgency of the message.

"Okay, okay, tell him I'll be there in a couple of minutes." Morris sat up to shake off the drowsiness of his nap. He looked over at the patio table next to him. His iced lemonade was still nearly full, and all of the ice cubes had melted. He stared at a large bead of condensation that slowly trickled down the side of the glass, at times pausing and then taking unexpected turns slowing and speeding up. He thought to himself, *Does that little bead know where it's going? Is something directing it, or is its journey just random?*

He became hypnotized watching the little droplet finally come to rest on the surface of the table. The intense heat of the afternoon made him groggy.

"Uncle Morris! Papa says if you don't come now we'll miss our flight."

Morris rubbed his eyes, jumped off the chaise lounge, and yelled back, "Okay, Jonas, tell him I'm coming!"

As he walked into the house, Jonas stopped him and held up a blue knapsack. "See, Uncle, I'm ready. Do you think I can play with my video game on the plane?"

"Once we're up in the air, I think you can. Are all your clothes packed?" Morris asked.

"Yep, Papa put 'em in the suitcase."

"Okay, let me go up and get ready. Don't get your clothes dirty now. We've got a long day ahead of us."

Morris ran upstairs to where Ephram was finishing up the packing. He snuck up behind him and gave him a kiss on the back of the neck. Ephram jumped and then playfully threw a pair of underwear at him.

Ephram had laid out Morris's travel clothes for him on the bed.

After a quick shower, Morris got dressed and put a few final items in one of the suitcases.

He and Ephram brought the four bulging suitcases down to the front hallway. They sat on the stairs by the front door for a moment to catch their breath. Ephram wrapped his arm around Morris's waist. He pointed to a sticker in the window by the front door. It said, "Our boy is an honor student." They exchanged looks of parental pride. They were raising Jonas well.

They had been anticipating their trip for a long time. Their excitement was tempered by cautious optimism that they were doing the right thing. Ephram stood up and paced while they waited for the cab to pick them up.

Before long the three of them were rushing out the front door to a waiting taxi. With their suitcases loaded in the trunk, they jumped in the backseat. Morris asked the driver to wait a moment. He looked out the window at the "Sold" sign hanging on a post in the front lawn. He stared momentarily with a blank expression and then slowly cracked a smile as the taxi sped away.

They arrived at the airport with a little time to spare, so they grabbed a sandwich and some snacks. Little Jonas was playing with his handheld video game and asking a lot of questions.

"Uncle Morris, will they feed us on the plane? Can I buy a candy bar to take with me?"

Morris gave Jonas money to go buy a candy bar. When he returned he held out his hand containing the change, a quarter and a penny. He gave the quarter to Morris and threw the penny on the ground.

Jonas looked up and signed as he spoke, "Maybe someone will pick up my penny and make a wish. Then their dream will come true."

Morris looked at Ephram and signed, "Just like his father." Ephram smiled.

After a few minutes, there was an announcement that their flight was ready for boarding.

Morris tapped Ephram on the shoulder. They gathered their carry-on bags and waited eagerly in line at the gate.

As they entered the plane, Morris paused and tapped Jonas on the shoulder and said, "Jonas, don't you have something to give the flight crew?"

Jonas replied, "Oh, yeah, Uncle Morris. Should I give it to them now?"

Morris nodded.

Jonas dug into his little knapsack and pulled out a large bag of Ghirardelli chocolates. He handed it to the flight attendant at the doorway and said, "Ma'am, this is for all the crew members. My uncle said you like to eat chocolate."

The surprised attendant reached down and gave Jonas a hug and told him, "Why thank you, young man. We certainly appreciate this, and we'll make sure you have a great flight."

Morris hadn't expected little Jonas to add that final comment, but he just smiled when the attendant looked up at him.

192 | RJ Stastny

Jonas giggled at the attention, but Morris motioned for him to move down the aisle to take their seats.

Ephram took the aisle seat because of his long legs. Morris took the middle, only because Jonas wanted to look out the window.

The gentleman across the aisle was busy typing on his laptop. His fingers were moving so quickly you could hear the clicking of the keys among the commotion of people boarding. Little Jonas stared for a few moments.

He leaned over Morris and said, "Hey, sir, what are you writing?"

Not appearing at all bothered, the man turned and said, "Just notes from a business meeting. Nothing interesting."

Jonas persevered, "Are you a writer?"

The man chuckled and stopped typing on his computer. "Not yet, but maybe someday."

Morris could only stare ahead and chuckle to himself.

Suddenly, he felt his phone vibrate. He had forgotten to turn it off before boarding. The text message read, "Congratulations on your book. Remember, you owe it all to me! The eighty-year-old girl is still kickin'! See you soon!"

Morris showed the message to Ephram, who was holding a book on his lap. On the cover there was a sticker that said, "Newly Released." The title was *Knowing Where You're Supposed to Be,* by Maurice Summerlin.

Morris reached over to his lap and turned the book over. On the back was a poem.

Dream until Real

If freed spirits are moved by what if,
The curious by why not,
If the explorer is driven by unrest,
The brave by unwilling to stop,

Then dreams are born by those who imagine,
They embrace those who believe,
They're achieved by risks to heart and soul,
With no rest until they're real.

—Maurice Summerlin

Morris pointed to the last line of the poem and signed to Ephram, "We're not ready to rest."

Ephram rubbed the back of Morris's neck and smiled.

The huge jet had taxied to the end of the runway. Morris reached to hold Ephram's hand on his left and Jonas's hand on his right. It was a night flight. The cabin lights had dimmed except for a few of the overhead lights, including those above Ephram and Morris. Morris wondered what his bright-red hair next to Ephram's graying curls must look like under the bright light. *Fire and ice.* He chuckled to himself.

Morris felt himself thrown back against his seat as the four engines of the 747 revved up to full power, propelling the beast of a plane down the runway. He took a deep breath, inhaling the signature airplane air that usually triggered anxiety. But today, instead of rattling his nerves, it had a more pleasant association.

With his head pressed against the seat, Morris turned to look at Ephram, who glanced back in his direction. Morris gazed directly into those large dark eyes, which at one time many years ago looked mysterious and foreboding. Today they were sparkling.

The roar of the engines grew louder, and the vibrations of the jet racing down the runway shook the overhead compartments. Morris could hear bottles and glasses clanging in the galley just behind him.

The jumbo jet lifted off the ground. Morris felt something by his feet. His personal bag had slid out from beneath his seat. The stylish leather mailbag revealed some wear and tear, and because of a missing snap at the top something had fallen out and was lying on the floor.

He asked Jonas to pick it up. Jonas unbuckled his seat belt, reached down and grabbed it, and quickly rebuckled his seat belt. His little hands held on tightly to the very old and mystical-looking book. There were small scratches on its carved wood cover and the thick leather binding had begun to crack at the seam. Despite the scratches and nicked corners, the green inlay of a flying dragon on the cover was spared the ravages of time. The rose-colored stone set in the middle was still clear and shiny. The gold edges of the pages shimmered in the dim light. Protruding from between one of the pages was a dried daylily, crumbling but still intact.

With his eyes wide open, he held up the book to Morris and Ephram. A knowing smile spread across Morris's face.

Morris signed to Ephram, "We're finally going home, Pacha."

He then turned to Jonas and whispered, "Yes, Little J. We're going home to Asilomar. It's where we're supposed to be."

END